"Put me
through

Nathan was probably trying to play her, to use her to his advantage the same way that Stephan had. That's what men like him did.

"Then tell me what you'll be doing on Friday," he demanded softly.

"Once you pick up the shipment from the airport, my part in this will be over."

"And then?"

She swallowed against the lump in her throat. "Then I'm going to sing."

He set her down on the top of the drum and caught her face in his hands. "I'd like to hear you, Kelly."

"Nathan..."

"I mean really hear you, when you're not holding back. I'd like to see the woman you are when you're not working for Volski, the one with the passion and the pain that you try so hard to hide."

"Stop it, Nathan. Just leave me alone."

"I can't."

"Why not?"

He moved his finger beneath her eye. It came away wet. He rubbed the moisture against his thumb. "That's why not."

Dear Reader,

June brings you six high-octane reads from Silhouette Intimate Moments, just in time for summer. First up, Ingrid Weaver enthralls readers with *Loving the Lone Wolf* (#1369), which is part of her revenge-ridden PAYBACK miniseries. Here, a street thug turned multimillionaire on a mission falls for the enemy's girlfriend and learns that looks can be deceiving! Crank up your air-conditioning as Debra Cowan's miniseries THE HOT ZONE will definitely raise temperatures with its firefighter characters. The second book, *Melting Point* (#1370), has a detective heroine and firefighting hero discovering more than one way to put out a fire as they track a serial killer.

Caridad Piñeiro lures us back to her haunting miniseries, THE CALLING. In *Danger Calls* (#1371), a beautiful doctor loses herself in her work, until a heady passion creates delicious chaos while throwing her onto a dangerous path. You'll want to curl up with Linda Winstead Jones's latest book, *One Major Distraction* (#1372), from her miniseries LAST CHANCE HEROES, in which a marine poses as a teacher to find a killer and falls for none other than the fetching school cook...who hides one whopper of a secret.

When a SWAT hero butts heads with a plucky reporter, a passionate interlude is sure to follow in Diana Duncan's *Truth or Consequences* (#1373), the next book in her fast-paced miniseries FOREVER IN A DAY. In *Deadly Reunion* (#1374), by Lauren Nichols, our heroine thinks her life is comfortable. But of course, mayhem ensues as her ex-husband—a man she's never stopped loving—returns to solve a murder and clear his name...and she's going to help him.

This month is all about finding love against the odds and those adventures lurking around the corner. So as you lounge in your favorite chair, lose yourself in one of these gems from Silhouette Intimate Moments!

Sincerely,

Patience Smith
Associate Senior Editor

Please address questions and book requests to:
Silhouette Reader Service
U.S.: 3010 Walden Ave., P.O. Box 1325, Buffalo, NY 14269
Canadian: P.O. Box 609, Fort Erie, Ont. L2A 5X3

INGRID
WEAVER

Loving the
Lone Wolf

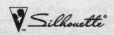
Silhouette®

INTIMATE MOMENTS™

Published by Silhouette Books

America's Publisher of Contemporary Romance

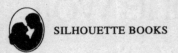 **SILHOUETTE BOOKS**

ISBN 0-373-27439-4

LOVING THE LONE WOLF

Copyright © 2005 by Ingrid Caris

All rights reserved. Except for use in any review, the reproduction
or utilization of this work in whole or in part in any form by any
electronic, mechanical or other means, now known or hereafter
invented, including xerography, photocopying and recording, or in
any information storage or retrieval system, is forbidden without
the written permission of the editorial office, Silhouette Books,
233 Broadway, New York, NY 10279 U.S.A.

All characters in this book have no existence outside the imagination of
the author and have no relation whatsoever to anyone bearing the same
name or names. They are not even distantly inspired by any individual
known or unknown to the author, and all incidents are pure invention.

This edition published by arrangement with Harlequin Books S.A.

® and TM are trademarks of Harlequin Books S.A., used under license.
Trademarks indicated with ® are registered in the United States Patent
and Trademark Office, the Canadian Trade Marks Office and in other
countries.

Visit Silhouette Books at www.eHarlequin.com

Printed in U.S.A.

Books by Ingrid Weaver

Silhouette Intimate Moments

True Blue #570
True Lies #660
On the Way to a Wedding... #761
Engaging Sam #875
What the Baby Knew #939
Cinderella's Secret Agent #1076
Fugitive Hearts #1101
Under the King's Command #1184
*Eye of the Beholder #1204
*Seven Days to Forever #1216
*Aim for the Heart #1258
In Destiny's Shadow #1329
†The Angel and the Outlaw #1352
†Loving the Lone Wolf #1369

Silhouette Special Edition

The Wolf and the Woman's Touch #1056

*Eagle Squadron
†Payback

Silhouette Books

Family Secrets
The Insider

INGRID WEAVER

admits to being a sucker for old movies and books that can make her cry. "I write because life is an adventure," Ingrid says. "And the greatest adventure of all is falling in love." Since the publication of her first book in 1994, she has won the Romance Writers of America RITA® Award for Romantic Suspense, as well as the *Romantic Times* Career Achievement Award for Series Romantic Suspense. Ingrid lives with her husband and son and an assortment of shamefully spoiled pets in a pocket of country paradise an afternoon's drive from Toronto. She invites you to visit her Web site at www.ingridweaver.com.

Prologue

"Mommy, look at this!"

The scene unfolded with the slow-motion horror of a nightmare. At first, Kelly couldn't accept what she was seeing. This was Jamie's playroom, part of their sanctuary, an island of sanity where her son could be just a kid and she could be simply a mom. Toy cars littered the carpet, crayons and paper covered the child-size desk and the cushions from the biggest couch had been propped into a pile on the floor to make a garage.

But Jamie wasn't holding a crayon or a car or the favorite threadbare stuffed rabbit that he had crawled into his couch-cushion garage to find.

He was holding a gun.

No. Oh, God, *no!*

The nightmare image continued to expand, melding the ordinary with the obscene. Under the eerily unblinking gaze of the toys that lined the shelves, sunlight glinted from the silver pistol, the same sunlight that sifted through Jamie's strawberry-blond hair and gilded the freckles on his cherub cheeks with gold.

Kelly fought to stay calm, despite the scream that swelled in her throat. She couldn't risk startling him. She unfolded her legs from where she had been sitting cross-legged on the floor. Holding out her hand, she knee-walked across the carpet. She was only two yards away. It seemed like two miles. "Jamie, please put that down."

The gun was a 9mm clip-loading semiautomatic, the kind the guards who patrolled the estate carried. It was too large for a three-year-old's tiny hands, so Jamie gripped the pistol by its barrel the same way he would normally grip the handle of the plastic hammer that had come with his toy tool bench. Oblivious to the danger, he sat back on his heels and tilted his head to investigate his new find. "Pow, pow!"

"Now, baby." Kelly halted in front of him, reached for the weapon and eased it from his hands. "Give it to Mommy."

"I want to play with it!"

The moment the gun was securely in Kelly's grip, her breath rushed out. Her pulse was pounding so hard, her chest ached. The urge to scream was getting stronger. It was almost as powerful as the urge to run.

Yes, run. Take her baby and keep going until her feet bled and her legs collapsed and there was no more air in her lungs. End the madness, leave the nightmare behind and find somewhere free and safe and normal where love wasn't a tool, armed men didn't patrol the halls and guns didn't end up between couch cushions like stray pocket change.

Her fingers trembled as she unloaded the gun and put it on the floor behind her. How it had gotten here, who had left it, were questions she would deal with later. She leaned over to pull her son into a hard embrace. Pressing her nose to his hair, she drew in his scent, that sweet mixture of baby shampoo and warm child, the familiar anchor for her senses when the world spun out of control....

Before she realized what she was doing, she was on her feet with her son clasped in her arms and was halfway across the room.

Kelly's scream emerged as a moan. Clenching her teeth, she stopped short of the door and turned in a circle. She couldn't run. Not yet. If she did, Stephan would track them down as he had before.

She had to be patient and stick to her plan. She had to use her head instead of her heart. She couldn't trust her heart. That's what had gotten her into this in the first place.

But, oh, God! If she had been three yards away instead of two, if Jamie had played with that gun instead of showing it to her, if he had looked down the barrel, if he had touched the trigger...

Kelly's shoulders shook with a sob. She sank to her knees, clutching Jamie to her chest. He squirmed, restless with his mother's need to cling, but she only hugged him tighter.

"I'll get us out of this," she whispered. "I promise."

The vow was one she had made countless times.

Only this time, she knew exactly how she would make it happen.

Chapter 1

Nathan Beliveau wasn't looking for a woman. Even if he had been, it sure as hell wouldn't have been this one.

From the improbable shade of her strawberry-blond hair to the lethal spikes of her stiletto heels, Kelly Jennings spelled trouble. She had the kind of presence that commanded the stage, drawing every gaze in the place as she posed in the spotlight. Her dress shimmered in a sheath of gold, caressing her body in a way that was designed to make any man there think about reaching out for those curves and doing the same.

But word on the street had it that this woman belonged to Stephan Volski. She was one of his trophies, a symbol of the Russian's power and his wealth, so only a suicidal fool would consider getting any part of his body even close to hers.

Ice cubes tinkled as Nathan wrapped his fingers

around his glass and leaned back in his chair. The lights dimmed until pinpoints of white shone from the ceiling like a network of stars. That's what Volski had named the nightclub, the Starlight.

It was a high-class place, one of the most popular in Chicago, with plush blue velvet covering the chairs and white linen on the small tables. A staff of polite servers glided unobtrusively around the room, although Nathan had spotted several who had the telltale bulge of a shoulder holster under their jackets. More muscle was positioned near the exits, but they kept their presence low-key. The majority of the patrons who frequented the club weren't aware this place was a front for the owner's real business. They came here for the ambiance and for the music.

Nathan had come here to settle a debt.

There was a scattering of applause as Kelly stepped up to the microphone. She acknowledged it with a graceful dip of her chin. Nathan couldn't see the color of her eyes from where he sat—he'd chosen a table far from the stage so he could put his back against the wall while keeping track of the people who entered the room—but he was still close enough to see that the rest of her features projected the same kind of sensuality as her body.

Her face was a classic oval, framed by an artful tumble of curls. Her high cheekbones and her generous mouth were emphasized by dramatic makeup, but she wore no jewelry around her neck. The tempting expanse of cleavage her dress revealed didn't need adornment.

When it came to choosing his trophies, Volski had spectacular taste. Kelly appeared to be made for pleasure, a woman who was well aware of her sex appeal and knew how to use it.

And fool or not, Nathan wasn't immune to her effect. He tried to ignore the stirring of interest he felt. It usually took more than a good body and a pretty face for him to notice a woman—he was more interested in what lay inside than in the packaging. Yet he couldn't deny that the mere sight of Kelly was getting to him.

It was an understandable response, a healthy male reaction to the display of a ripe female.

Nathan reminded himself once again that this was the wrong female.

He sipped his drink and surveyed the crowd, turning his thoughts back to business. Volski's emissary was supposed to have been here five minutes ago. It had taken Nathan over a month to set up this meeting, and Tony's patience was running out. The plan was still a good one, though. All he needed was the chance to put it into motion.

A glimmer of movement drew his gaze back to the stage. Kelly's dress shifted as she curled her fingers around the microphone, revealing another half inch of cleavage. Contrary to what Nathan expected, her full lips didn't curve with the smile of a seductress. Instead, they thinned with determination. She remained motionless, as if she were drawing into herself. It went on so long, the audience began to grow restive. Finally, she closed her eyes, lifted her face and began to sing.

If Nathan hadn't already been leaning his chair against the wall, he would have been knocked on his butt by her first note.

Longing. Pain.

Rage.

The emotions that trembled through the air were so genuine, so raw, that Nathan felt as if he'd been struck.

This wasn't an act. What Kelly was doing on that stage was too private, making it seem as if he were intruding merely by listening.

He wasn't alone. The entire audience went silent, as if they were as stunned by the intimacy of what they were hearing as Nathan was. The melody was familiar, an old torch song from the 1930s, yet Kelly made it sound as if it had been written just for her.

There were musicians backing her up, a jazz trio consisting of a pianist, a bass player and a drummer. Nathan could see their silhouettes on the stage beyond the range of the spotlight, yet they kept their contribution to the music as unobtrusive as their appearance. Kelly's voice didn't need adornment any more than her features did.

Nathan swallowed the rest of his drink, along with a pang of regret. There had to be more to Kelly than just the packaging. How did a woman who sang like this, whose performance hinted at such depth to her emotions, end up involved with scum like Stephan Volski?

Maybe the rumors were wrong.

Damn, he hoped so.

Because if Kelly Jennings was anywhere near her boyfriend when this deal went down, she would be trading her stage for a prison cell.

This would be the last time, the very last time, that Kelly would negotiate a deal for Stephan. All she had to do was set this business into motion and she and Jamie would be as good as gone. The smuggler she had been sent to meet was about to become their ticket to freedom.

Yet even knowing that, Kelly still felt her stomach

rebel as she stepped off the stage. She paused to smooth her dress until the queasiness passed, then put on her best performer's smile and kept her gaze on the back wall as she moved between the tables. She didn't waste time by going backstage to change. That would be an indulgence she couldn't afford. She'd already indulged herself enough for one night.

What had come over her? How could she have exposed her feelings that way? The past three years had taught her better than that. It was enough that she exposed half her bosom without laying bare her heart.

She should have restrained herself as she always did. Put on a show, gone through the motions, given the audience what they expected so everyone went home happy. Yet her control had been stretched to the limit today. The frustrated rage she'd kept inside since she had seen that gun in Jamie's hands had needed to be released. Music was the only safe outlet she had. Without it, she likely would have gone insane by now.

But the respite was over. Rand was already here. One of Stephan's watchdogs had pointed him out to her as soon as the set had ended.

He sat alone at a table in the shadows, his chair casually tipped back against the wall. He'd extinguished the candle that had burned in the glass bowl on the table, so she couldn't yet see his face, but she could feel his gaze on her as she worked her way closer.

Fine. She knew how to handle that. If Rand was like most of Stephan's associates, he'd be too busy ogling her to realize he was about to be played. She decided to put on a show for him, too, and give him what he expected. She added a hint of extra sway to her hips.

This had to work. She couldn't let herself think of what she might be driven to do if it didn't.

She paused when she reached his table, inhaled from the diaphragm to calm her nerves and held out her hand. "Hello, Mr. Rand," she said, deliberately pitching her voice low so that he would have to draw closer in order to hear. "I'm Kelly Jennings. Sorry to keep you waiting."

He hesitated briefly before he rose to his feet. He was a tall man. Despite the four-inch heels Kelly wore, her eyes were only on a level with his chin. A loosely knotted tie hung from the open collar of his white shirt, likely a token concession to the Starlight's dress code, but the jacket that stretched across his wide shoulders was biker black leather. It creaked as he extended his arm to take her hand. "I wasn't expecting Volski's man to be a woman," he said.

The deep voice went along with his size. It was as masculine as the scent of leather and the hint of spicy aftershave that rose with him. She cranked up the wattage of her smile. "I hope you're not disappoint—"

She never finished the inane comment. The first touch of his palm against her own stole her breath. Maybe it was due to anxiety, or maybe it was a result of fatigue, but when he closed his fingers around hers, she felt a thrill chase across her nerves.

His hand was large, his fingers long and tanned. The strength in his grip was wrapped in a gentleness that was at odds with his size and his choice of wardrobe. Kelly lifted her gaze from his hand to his face.

Good Lord, she thought. Whatever crimes this man did for a living, whatever he was on the inside, there was no denying that the outside was gorgeous. He had a square jaw and broad cheekbones, with a bold hawklike nose that evoked the image of a native warrior. His jet-black hair was cut short and combed straight back from his forehead, but he would have looked just as good with it long and braided. She could picture him on horseback, his shoulders clad in buckskin and his chiseled face bathed by moonlight...

"*Surprised* would be more accurate," he murmured.

Kelly blinked, wrenching her mind back to business. What was wrong with her tonight? Rand's appearance meant nothing to her. She wasn't looking for a man. She was looking for a patsy, a sucker. A scapegoat. She gestured to the chair beside his. "Well, I hope you mean that in a good way. Do you mind if I join you?"

He held her chair for her. It wasn't a showy courtesy, it seemed to come naturally to him. He resumed his seat, picked up a book of matches from the table and lit the candle.

His eyes were the color of amber, reflecting the flame with flecks of gold. And despite her revealing neckline, he kept his gaze on her face. "I have what you need," he said quietly.

How right he was, she thought. "That sounds promising. Would you care to elaborate?"

"I'm in the transportation business. Volski's looking for a new method to move his product. The math seems simple enough."

"We checked out your background, Mr. Rand. We heard you ran a successful operation in Detroit ten years ago, but your experience was limited to stealing cars."

"I prefer to regard it as redistributing them."

"That's an interesting way to put it."

"It's accurate. I either broke them down for parts or shipped them overseas."

"Yes, so I heard. You had a good reputation." She maintained her smile as she continued to scrutinize him. "But you dropped out of sight. Why is it that no one seems to have heard of you since then?"

"Because I've moved up from stealing cars, and I'm very good at what I do."

"And that is?"

"I told you. Transportation."

She crossed her arms on the table and angled her shoulders toward him. Cool air wafted across her breasts as her neckline gaped. She didn't pull back—she wanted to put him off balance and she would take any advantage she could get. "You must understand why we would be concerned. Your timely arrival seems too convenient. We need to be sure you are what you claim to be."

"Sorry, I wasn't aware you would require references. I left my résumé in my other suit." A muscle in his jaw twitched. Still keeping his gaze on hers, he moved the candleholder aside. "You might want to be careful where you lean. That dress looks combustible."

"Do you like it?"

"If I say yes, is it going to help our negotiations or hurt them?"

This was going to be tougher than she thought. She let her smile fade. "Perhaps you could explain why we should trust you, Mr. Rand."

"That goes both ways, Miss Jennings."

"Oh, please. There's no need to be so formal. Call me Kelly."

"Let's quit playing games, Kelly. Volski must already trust me or he wouldn't have arranged this meeting."

"He's interested, yes, but—"

"But he sent you to distract me so he can negotiate a better deal."

Normally, that would be true. Stephan had recognized her potential from the start and had been quick to exploit it, but this time it was her own agenda, not his, that had her pulling out all the stops. "Nathan," she began. She splayed her hand on the bare skin at the base of her throat in a gesture that was a surefire attention getter. "I may call you Nathan, may I not?"

He touched his index finger to her knuckle, then traced his way down the back of her hand until he rested his fingertip on the upper curve of her breast. Incredibly, his gaze still didn't waver from hers. "You can call me whatever you like, Kelly, as long as it doesn't include fool. I'm here for business, and regardless of what you're trying to accomplish with this lovely display—" he pressed lightly, stroking her breast along the edge of her little finger "—I believe you're here for business, too."

She had to exercise every ounce of her control to stay in character and keep from jerking back. Not because someone might see them and report this to Stephan— with her back to the room and the table positioned in the shadows, no one else would be aware of Nathan's caress. And not because the contact repulsed her. It was quite the opposite. His touch on her breast wasn't invasive, it was tender, almost…regretful. This was as unexpected as the thrill she'd felt from his handshake and so help her, despite what she knew about him, she found it pleasant.

That was why it had to end. This wasn't what she had planned. Just who was distracting whom? She eased her shoulders back, reducing the contact until all she could feel was the warmth from his fingertip.

"I have what you need," he repeated. "I have a network in place that can move the merchandise Volski has stockpiled in Vladivostok." He withdrew his hand, ending the caress as casually as he had started it. He crossed his arms. "The only question here is if you can make it worth my while."

Her skin tingled where he had touched her. Beneath it, her heart started to pound. This was the opportunity she had been waiting for. She fought to keep her eagerness from showing. "You seem like an intelligent man, Nathan. Intelligent and ambitious. I like that."

"And you sing as if there's a hell of a lot more to you than you're pretending, Kelly. I'm not sure whether I like that or not."

This time she did jerk. His touch on her body was one thing, but that comment was just too personal. Pretending? God, he couldn't possibly know the truth. "I'm glad you enjoyed the show."

"Was that what it was?"

"Why, of course. I'm a singer. That's what I do."

"No, what you *do* is work for Volski. From what I heard on that stage tonight, singing is what you are."

Damn, his insight was right on target. It appeared that she had underestimated him. She had to wrap this up before he sliced any deeper. "Then on behalf of Stephan, I have a proposal to present."

"I'm listening."

"Since we haven't worked together before, we must overcome trust issues on both sides. The best way to do that is to increase the stakes."

"How?"

"Rather than accepting a flat fee up front for your services, I'm proposing that you take a percentage of the profits once the merchandise is sold."

He raised his eyebrows. "A percentage? Why?"

"Insurance. Stephan doesn't want a one-off—he wants an ongoing relationship. If you fail to move the goods as you promise, then you won't make anything, but if you succeed, your profit will be tied to ours."

"Uh-huh. And if you don't make a profit—"

"Oh, we'll make a profit, Nathan." She slid her hand along her breast and under the neckline of her dress until the tips of her fingers slipped into her bra. "Let me show you a sample of what I'm offering."

His arm shot out across the table. His touch wasn't gentle this time as he clamped his fingers around her wrist to hold her hand in place. The flame that was reflected in his eyes flared dangerously. "Kelly…"

The warning in his voice was plain—she had pushed the game as far as he would allow—but she wasn't playing now. She twisted her hand so that he could see the small, condom-size packet that she had taken from her bra.

He exhaled hard enough to make the candle waver. Muttering an oath, he released her wrist.

Kelly turned the packet between her fingers. The clear plastic didn't hold a prophylactic. It held a tablespoon of fine white powder.

It was pure, uncut heroin, gram for gram, one of the most valuable commodities on the planet. It was the primary source of Stephan's wealth, and being this close to it was making Kelly want to throw up, but she did some more deep breathing until the urge passed.

Almost there, she told herself. She had put out the bait. Now it was only a question of how fast he would take it.

Nathan plucked the heroin from her grasp and closed it in his fist so tightly his knuckles paled.

Good, she thought. Until now, his expression had been unreadable, but his body language betrayed him. This deal appeared to be almost as important to him as it was to her. "It's yours to keep," Kelly said. "I believe you'll want to test it."

"I intend to."

"There are two more tons where this came from, Nathan. Your share would make you a rich man."

The mention of the amount of heroin didn't appear to move him. Nor did the prospect of riches. He slipped the dope into a pocket on the front of his jacket and zipped it closed. "What kind of percentage did Volski have in mind?"

"That's what I'm here to negotiate."

He regarded her steadily. "Name a number."

"First I need to see what you have to offer." Kelly pinched the shoulders of her dress and hitched it back into place. "Now that I've shown you mine," she murmured, "it's your turn to show me yours."

Chapter 2

Nathan had thought the ride would do him good. That's why whenever he could he preferred to use his bike instead of his customized Jaguar. There was nothing like the molar-jarring vibration from a Harley's split carburetor and the slam of night air at seventy miles an hour to help clear a man's head. Traffic on the expressway was light at this hour so he'd been able to open up the throttle the instant he'd cleared the ramp.

But it wasn't working. How could he clear his head when every square inch of his body was humming with awareness?

Kelly was nestled behind him, her hands clasped around his waist and her thighs cradling his hips. Even through his jacket he could feel the pressure of her breasts as she squeezed against his back to shelter from the wind.

At least she'd changed out of that damn dress. Otherwise, he wouldn't have had a hope of getting this far. Had she realized what she'd been doing to him?

Yes. Absolutely. She'd known full well how to use her sexuality to her advantage. She thought she could manipulate him by leading him around by his libido. It was all part of her strategy.

It bothered the hell out of him to realize how effective it had been.

He clenched his jaw and twisted his wrist, accelerating to pass a slow-moving truck. Kelly leaned with him as he changed lanes, her body locked to his. He had assumed she would choose to postpone this part of their business until later, but she seemed as anxious to put the deal into motion as he was. She hadn't balked when she had seen the motorcycle. Instead, she had told him to wait, then had reappeared outside the Starlight fifteen minutes later dressed in flat-heeled shoes, tailored pants and a modest sweater, a helmet she had borrowed from one of the club's bouncers in her hand.

Her sensible outfit hadn't done much to disguise her figure, especially since the way she was plastered to him now let Nathan feel even more than the dress had allowed him to see.

But that was probably all part of her game, too. Her determination was as formidable an asset as her body. Volski had chosen his emissary—and his trophy—well.

Right. Volski.

Nathan checked his speed and eased back on the throttle to bring it under the limit. Getting stopped by the cops at this stage was the last thing he needed. He had a bag of pure heroin in the pocket of his jacket and he had the girlfriend of a notorious Russian drug kingpin on the back of his bike. On top of that, he was using a name he hadn't gone by for a decade.

What Kelly had learned about his past had been accurate. Ten years ago, Nathan Rand had run the most successful chop shop in Detroit. His network of car thieves had stretched from Michigan across the border to Ontario, targeting only high-end vehicles. His staff had been skilled and highly motivated, all pros like him. He'd been investigated by police forces in both countries and he'd been arrested three times, but he'd always beaten the charges. As he'd told Kelly, he was good at what he did.

But what Kelly didn't know—and what Volski could never find out—was the real reason Nathan Rand had dropped out of sight. He had relocated from Detroit to Chicago and had become Nathan Beliveau, the president and CEO of what was now the third-largest courier company in the nation.

Nathan's current network stretched not only around the Great Lakes but throughout North America. Every vehicle his company owned had been acquired honestly. Instead of working under the threat of prison time, his skilled, highly motivated staff could look forward to medical benefits and a generous pension plan. He had transformed himself from an international car thief to an upstanding, taxpaying citizen.

So what he'd told Kelly had been accurate, too. He was indeed in the transportation business. He was proud of the new life he'd built, but it hadn't come cheap. Unless he paid his debt to Tony Monaco, he could lose it all.

The reminder focused his thoughts better than the ride could. He took the exit for O'Hare Airport, switched off his headlight and headed for the back route he liked to use. Seven minutes later, they arrived at the sprawling complex of warehouses and hangars that bore the gray-and-white baying-wolf logo of Pack Leader Express.

It's your turn to show me yours.

Showing Kelly what he had to offer was exactly what he intended to do. That was why he was about to go through the charade of breaking into the head office of his own company.

Nathan coasted to a stop in the shadows outside the chain-link fence that ran behind the Pack Leader main warehouse. Security was tight in the freight-handling areas, so he planned to stick to the administrative building. He pulled back his cuff to check his watch, then shut off the engine.

Kelly unclasped her hands from his waist. "Why are we stopping here?" she asked.

He set the kickstand, slipped off his helmet and twisted on the seat to look at her. "I know the security guards' schedule. They pass through the main parking lot a few times a night, but there's no entrance back here for them to check so they won't notice my bike."

She lifted off her helmet and fluffed her hair with her fingers. A whiff of floral-scented shampoo mingled with the exhaust from the bike. "What about surveillance cameras?"

"They're focused on the entrances and on the loading bays. This is a dead spot."

She surveyed the area. "I'm impressed by how you've studied the security, Nathan, but it still doesn't show me how you propose to move our merchandise."

He swung his leg over the gas tank, got to his feet and held out his hand. "Come with me."

She slid off the bike, hesitating for a telling moment before she slipped her hand into his.

Nathan knew it was crazy to feel a shock from the contact, since he'd felt her body rubbing and jiggling against him for the past half hour, yet the sensation of her skin pressed to his made his mouth go dry.

She didn't need stage makeup or a sequined dress to get to him. Although the shadows were deep here, he could feel the impact of her gaze. Her eyes were the vibrant green of springtime, fresh with life and hinting at earthy passion that was still tightly coiled.

Did she save her passion only for her singing? What would she do if he took her in his arms and eased her further into the shadows, pressed his mouth to her lips and her back to the wall and...

Damn, he had to keep his mind on business. He was taking a hell of a risk by bringing Kelly here, but it was the quickest way to cement this deal. Everything she saw and did was going to get straight back to Volski, so he had to put on the show of his life.

He tightened his grip on her hand and guided her across the tarmac to the small square building at the hub of the complex. The wolf logo was done in lights here, unlike the painted signs on the other buildings. He gave the glow from the sign a wide berth as he bypassed the main entrance and led Kelly to a door that was set in the middle of the side wall. Angling his body so that she wouldn't be able to see what he did, he went through the motions of jimmying the lock, then punched in the combination on the keypad, opened the door and tugged her inside.

As he'd anticipated, the corridor was empty. Most of the people who worked the midnight shift would be monitoring activity from the communication center at the front of the building. If someone did happen to see him using his private entrance, they wouldn't find his presence here unusual—Nathan didn't sleep much, and he preferred a hands-on style of management, so he often wandered the complex at night.

But if Kelly heard someone address him by the name he used now, the game with Volski would be over almost before it had begun.

She opened her mouth as if she were about to ask another question, but he silenced her by shaking his head and holding his finger to her lips. He leaned down to put his mouth close to her ear. "We'll go upstairs," he whispered. "You can see the entire layout from there. It's safer than going around to the warehouse."

She nodded and one of her curls tickled his nose.

His eyes half closed as he inhaled. There was the floral shampoo, feminine and sensuous, but beneath it there was a hint of something sweet. A mild, powdery aroma that was oddly...innocent.

Longing, pain...rage.

The memory of her voice rose with her scent. The calculating woman who belonged to Stephan Volski wouldn't smell like this any more than she would be able to sing with so much emotion. Again, Nathan found himself thinking there had to be more to Kelly than what showed on the surface.

But that wasn't his concern, was it? He wasn't looking for a complication any more than he was looking for a woman. Kelly's only reason for being here with him was to negotiate a way to move her boyfriend's heroin.

As for Nathan's reason for being here with Kelly... well, they were standing in the middle of it.

He straightened up and led her to the stairs.

* * *

Nathan's nerves had to be made of steel, Kelly thought, crouching behind the low ridge of concrete that ran along the edge of the roof. And as for that other part of the male anatomy that supposedly went along with courage, he must have a pair of the largest, firmest—

She gritted her teeth, refusing to consider anything else about his body. She'd already felt plenty of it on the motorcycle trip here. Yes, thanks to that ride, she'd been treated to hands-on knowledge of his wide shoulders, his slim hips, his hard thighs and his broad chest. And she'd learned his scent was from more than leather and aftershave. He had the compelling, musky tang of a dangerously virile man.

"The shipment will get stored in that warehouse after it comes in," Nathan said. He squatted beside her and pointed toward a building to their right.

The airport spread out before them in a giant tapestry threaded with rows of lights. The terminal buildings were far enough away to look small, yet the well-lit complex of warehouses that surrounded them made Kelly feel uncomfortable. There was no cover here on the roof. If anyone decided to look in this direction, they would be spotted for sure.

But compared to the crimes Stephan had drawn her into, a little breaking, entering and trespassing were insignificant. Most of her anxiety arose from the fear that if they were caught here, the distribution deal would be blown and so would her and Jamie's escape plan.

She wiped her damp palms against her pants and turned her head to follow Nathan's gesture. She didn't want him to see her nervousness. It might give him an advantage.

"I didn't think to ask before," Nathan said. "Are you bothered by heights?"

His question sounded sincere, as did the note of concern in his voice, but Kelly couldn't be sure. Bringing her here might be a ploy to rattle her, the same way she'd been trying to rattle him before. "Not at all," she replied. "Besides, this building is hardly the Sears Tower."

"It's too close to a flight path to be any higher."

As if to prove his statement, his words were drowned out by the roar of a jet taking off. Kelly pressed her palms over her ears and instinctively ducked her head.

Nathan dropped to one knee and slipped his arm around her shoulders to steady her as the noise washed over them. Once it subsided, he didn't pull away immediately. He moved his fingers, toying briefly with the ends of her hair.

She told herself that she shouldn't feel anything from the caress. After all, it was only her hair that he touched. So why did she have this strange impulse to lean toward him for more?

Her jaw was starting to ache from clenching her teeth. It was a good thing that this was almost over.

He withdrew his hand and grasped the top of the concrete ledge. "The other courier companies go for small packets and speed," he said. "Pack Leader offers the same service, but specializes in bigger shipments. Loads are held in that warehouse, then get moved out as soon as a truck is available, usually within six hours."

"That suits us. The longer it sits, the more chance there is of someone getting curious about what's in it."

"How is it going to be packed?"

"What do you mean?"

"I heard Volski's last pipeline brought his junk in by stuffing it into outboard motor parts."

"That method was compromised. We'll be using something else."

"Which is?"

"Stephan will let you know when he feels it's necessary," Kelly said.

Nathan paused, then shifted closer. "Unless you level with me, this isn't going to work. I need to know the weight and dimensions of the shipment so that I can arrange the most efficient transportation."

"I understand. He'll give you the specifics ahead of time, but not yet." She inhaled slowly as the breeze brought her his scent. He was close enough for her to feel his body heat. Sexual awareness rippled down her spine. Was he doing this purposely, trying to turn the tables by using her own strategy on her?

What she had begun at the Starlight was backfiring. Instead of faking an interest in him, she had to convince herself that she *wasn't* interested. She tipped her head to follow the blinking lights of another plane. "You still haven't explained how this is going to go down."

"If I told you that, what would stop you from double-crossing me and using the information I give you to go with someone else?"

She was glad that she was already facing away from him, so she wouldn't have to worry about hiding her thoughts. He couldn't know how close to the truth he had come. "Don't you trust me, Nathan?"

"About as much as you trust me, Kelly."

He was surprisingly direct, different from the other criminals she'd met through Stephan. "Could someone else offer us what you can?" she asked.

"No one else has my particular connections."

"Then you have nothing to worry about. I've found that mutual interest is more reliable than mutual trust."

"So young, and so cynical," he murmured. "Is that why you save your passion for your music?"

Another direct hit, she thought. She had to finish this now. "As much as I'm enjoying all this witty repartee, Nathan, it's getting late," she said, pushing to her feet. "I'd like to proceed with our business."

He looked at her for a minute, his gaze hooded with shadows, then stood and led her to the other side of the roof.

A sea of trucks, all painted gray and white with the Pack Leader wolf logo, stretched out in a fenced yard below them. The sizes ranged from small delivery vans to eighteen-wheelers. As they watched, a man in the dark gray company uniform strode to a midsize van and drove it through the gate.

Nathan drew her back from the edge of the roof as the van passed by. "The best way to smuggle anything is in plain sight," he said.

"How?"

"All it takes to clear a load from customs is the right documentation. I know someone in the main office here who can create that with a few keystrokes."

"And then what?"

"We put it on a truck and drive it wherever you want it to go."

"It sounds too simple."

"It's the flaw of a big system. Pack Leader processes so many shipments daily that adding one more to the schedule won't make a ripple. One hand doesn't know what the other hand is doing. And the company is so well established, it's above suspicion."

"Aren't there tracking mechanisms?"

"Sure, there's an order number, but once it's in the system, there would be no reason for anyone except the client to access it," he said, raising his voice over the roar of another jet. He guided her back to the stairs that had brought them to the roof. "I've been transporting merchandise into the country by piggybacking it with legitimate goods for years. This company has been a gold mine, and the suits at the top don't even know it."

"But what about the driver? Wouldn't he have to be in on it?"

"In this case, I'll fix it so I would handle Volski's shipment personally."

"How?"

He didn't reply until they had stepped into the stairwell and the door had swung shut behind them, muffling the noise of the plane. "By putting on a uniform, walking into the yard and driving out with a truck."

She shook her head. "Stealing a truck would bring too much attention."

"I didn't say I would steal it."

"Then how will you get it?"

The light over the stairs was bright enough to reveal a glimmer of humor in his expression. "Easy. I work here."

Kelly stared. Was that a smile? It was only a shift of a few facial muscles, a soft crinkling of the skin at the corners of his eyes, a deepening of the lines beside his mouth, yet it hinted at a warmth she hadn't seen before. It was so at odds with his warrior demeanor that she found herself intrigued. What would it be like to see him smile fully, or maybe to hear him laugh?

Wait. What was that he had said? "You work here?" she asked.

"You're welcome to check that out, too. My name's on the Pack Leader payroll as a relief driver. There isn't a vehicle with wheels that I don't know how to handle."

Her mind clicked back on track as she evaluated the potential of his scheme.

One hand doesn't know what the other hand is doing.

This was exactly what she'd been looking for. She had enough information now to set the deal into motion.

She felt a stirring of regret over what would happen to this man when it was over, but she tried to ignore it. With Jamie's future at stake, she couldn't afford the luxury of a conscience.

She did her best to disregard the warmth she sensed in Nathan's almost-smile, too. It made no difference. After tonight, they would never see each other again.

It looked as if she had found the perfect scapegoat.

Although it was 2:00 a.m., the chandelier that hung in the three-story foyer of Stephan Volski's fortified mansion blazed with light. It was a monstrous piece, heavy with crystal and studded with gilded eagles that were ornate enough to belong in a czar's ballroom, which was where Stephan claimed it had originally hung. It was one of his prize possessions.

Kelly shuddered as she passed beneath it, her footsteps echoing on the marble floor. She knew that Stephan regarded her and Jamie as possessions, too. Prizes to be polished and put on display like his gaudy chandelier. They were tributes to his ego.

Sometimes she couldn't believe she had once been naive enough to think otherwise. Could she really have been that young? Had the innocent woman she remembered ever truly existed?

There was a metallic clunking noise from behind her, followed by a series of electronic beeps as the guard at the front door locked up and reset the alarm.

Kelly kept walking. She knew there was no point looking back. It hurt too much. The only way out of this was to go forward.

The door of Stephan's office was open when she reached it. Her shoes made no noise here—the hand-knotted carpet that covered the floor was thick enough to muffle a scream—so she took a moment to observe him in silence.

Despite the late hour, Stephan Volski was dressed in a light gray suit, his only allowance to comfort a slight loosening in the knot of his tie. His fine blond hair was neatly combed—he had it trimmed weekly. His elegantly handsome features and slender build gave him an air of sophistication. He appeared as harmless as a scholar as he bent his head over the papers that were scattered across his massive walnut desk.

Four years ago she had been dazzled by his charm, flattered by his attention and so hungry for love she hadn't wanted to see past it. He'd been her Prince Charming, riding to the rescue, sweeping her into a fairy-tale future. Their affair had lasted one month. By the time Kelly had realized that what she saw in Stephan was an illusion, a carefully cultivated veneer to hide the ugliness beneath, she was already carrying his child.

No, not *his* child, she thought, curling her nails into her palms. Jamie was hers. All hers. There was nothing of his father in him except for the pale blue eyes. Her son was kind and loving and sweet and innocent and...

Dear God, she had to get him away from here before that changed.

Stephan rubbed his eyes and lifted his head. He gave an involuntary start when he saw her. He scowled and pushed his chair back from his desk. "You're late."

When they were in private, Stephan made no pretense of affection toward her—he had moved on to other women well before his child had been born—yet it suited his pride to let people believe that Kelly was his.

It suited her, too, by providing her with protection. Because the men she had to deal with believed she was Stephan's girlfriend, they knew they could look but not touch.

Her true relationship with Stephan was a combination standoff and balancing act. As long as he had Jamie, Kelly would stay with Stephan, and as long as she stayed with Stephan, he would demand that she earn her keep by singing in his club and occasionally helping him with his business.

It astounded her that she had once thought his accent was romantic and his brooding silences were sensitive. How could she have allowed him to touch her?

Yet Nathan Rand was a criminal, just like Stephan. How on earth could she have found Nathan attractive? Why hadn't she found his touch repulsive?

Dammit, hadn't she learned anything?

"The meeting with Rand took longer than I expected." She walked past the fireplace with its carved marble mantel and gilded screen to the table that held an ornate silver samovar, another item that had supposedly belonged in an imperial palace. Moving mechanically, she drew a cup of steaming water and fixed herself some tea. Not that she had ever developed a taste for Russian tea, but she needed something to keep her hands busy. "I just got in."

"Tell me what happened."

She added some sugar to her cup and stirred while she gave Stephan a summary of what she had learned from Nathan. "I think we should look for someone else," she finished.

"Why?"

"Rand wants a percentage of our profits. He says it's insurance so he can trust us." She kept her gaze on her swirling tea. Stephan's only weaknesses were his pride and his paranoia, so the best way to get him to agree to something was to suggest the opposite. For the same reason, she didn't want him to know that giving Rand a percentage was her idea. It was insurance for her—without money up front, Rand would be less likely to bail on the deal.

"That would work in our favor," Stephan said. "I can delay paying him his share. What percentage does he want?"

"After I saw his setup, we settled on thirty-five."

Stephan pursed his lips as he considered that for a moment. Kelly guessed he was probably thinking of ways to cheat on the percentage. "We won't look for anyone else," he said finally. "We'll go with Rand."

She concentrated on keeping the spoon from rattling against the cup despite the sudden jump of her pulse. That had seemed too easy. Now for the next gambit. "I'm not sure we should trust him. He's very...contained."

"Are you losing your touch, Kelly?" Stephan lowered his voice slyly. "Or do Rand's preferences lie in another direction?"

The implication that Nathan wasn't heterosexual was so absurd, Kelly almost lost her concentration. The man put out pheromones that would be unmistakable to any female who possessed a pulse. She set the spoon down on the silver tray beneath the samovar. "Neither. He doesn't seem to want supervision."

"It's not his call. We have too many customers depending on this shipment. If Rand says he doesn't want supervision, he might have something to hide. We'll have to keep a close eye on him until my merchandise is delivered. I've decided to bring it in next Friday."

Kelly caught her breath. Friday? That was only a week away. In seven days, the nightmare would be over. And the seed of suspicion was planted. This was what she wanted. The pieces were falling into place better than she could have imagined.

Because while Stephan worried about trusting Nathan, and Nathan worried about trusting Stephan, Kelly planned to betray them both and disappear with Jamie.

The sheer daring of her plan terrified her. She knew how ruthless Stephan could be. If she failed to get away this time, she was certain she wouldn't get another opportunity. He tolerated her presence in Jamie's life because of their child's age, but if he suspected for an instant that she was planning to double-cross him, he had the wealth and connections to move Jamie someplace where she would never find him.

Her hands trembled at the thought. Tea slopped down the front of her pants and onto the carpet. She put down the cup and grasped her pant leg to hold the scalding liquid away from her skin.

Stephan rounded his desk and walked to her side. "Is something wrong, Kelly?" There was no concern in his voice, only irritation. "You seem on edge."

"It's been a long day and it's late."

"Do not lie to me." He narrowed his eyes. They were

the same height when she wore flat heels, so his gaze bored into hers. His eyes were so much like Jamie's, and yet so empty of warmth, the resemblance made her shudder. "I can see that something is troubling you," he said.

Kelly felt a bubble of hysteria. She was about to cheat an egomaniacal heroin czar, put the blame on a drug smuggler who looked like an Indian warrior and she was facing the rest of her life on the run from both of them with her child.

What could possibly be troubling her?

"I know what it is."

She pressed her tongue hard to the back of her front teeth, an old singer's trick to stem the panic reaction and force her body to relax. God, he couldn't know, could he? She'd been so careful.

"Gloria told me the boy got his hands on a gun."

It took a second to change gears. With everything else going on, Kelly had pushed that particular nightmare to the back of her mind. At Stephan's words, the image from this afternoon returned full force: Jamie in his playroom, his hair tousled as he backed out of the couch cushions, the sunlight gleaming from the pistol.

"You should have told me," Stephan said. "Instead I heard it from the nanny."

"You were busy," Kelly said. "And I had to leave for the Starlight."

"Simply because I do not spend as much time with our son as you do, don't think his welfare doesn't concern me. When he is old enough, he will be trained to take his place at my side."

Trained? The prospect chilled her to her bones. She couldn't let that happen. Whatever the cost, she had to get Jamie away before he fell under his father's influence. "I spoke to the guards," she said. She took a step back. "I told them not to bring their weapons into my and Jamie's suite."

"Pah!" He muttered a string of oaths in Russian. "That is not enough. I have dealt with it myself."

"How?"

He returned to his desk and pressed a button on his phone. "Dimitri? Where's Alex?"

A guttural, heavily accented voice came through the speaker. "In the basement, Mr. Volski."

"Bring him to my office now."

A few minutes later, the marble in the hall clattered with a set of heavy footsteps, along with a scuffing, thudding noise. The tall, blond Dimitri Petrovich, Stephan's lieutenant, entered the room with a burly, middle-aged man in tow.

It was Alex Almari, a veteran guard who also served as one of Stephan's enforcers. Kelly barely recognized him. His lower lip had been split open, the skin on his cheeks was raw from abrasions and his eyes were reduced to slits behind pulpy, purple swelling. He staggered a few steps sideways when Dimitri released his arm, then locked his knees and managed to stay on his feet.

Kelly pressed her fingers to her mouth. "Oh, my God. What happened to—"

"This is the imbecile who endangered the boy," Stephan said.

Kelly swallowed hard. When she had seen the weapon in Jamie's hands, she had been so shaken that if the person responsible for leaving the gun had been standing in front of her then, she probably would have struck him herself. She would do anything to protect her child.

But these injuries weren't the result of a parent's impulsive blow, they were from a methodical beating. Even though Alex Almari had probably inflicted far worse on others over the years, the sight of his face left Kelly sickened.

Stephan walked to the man and grabbed his chin to turn his face toward her. Fresh blood welled from Alex's lip and trickled onto Stephan's hand. "Do you not approve of my punishment, Kelly?"

"There shouldn't be any guns allowed near Jamie," she said. "That's the only sure way to prevent it from happening again."

"I prefer my way," Stephan said. He stepped back, taking a handkerchief from the breast pocket of his suit to wipe the smears of blood from his fingers. "Dimitri?"

"Yes, sir?"

"Take Alex outside and shoot him. Use his own gun."

"Stephan, no!" Kelly cried.

The gaze Stephan turned toward her froze her where she stood. "I value what's mine, Kelly. Anyone who threatens my son deserves no mercy."

"Please," Alex said. The burly enforcer's voice was distorted by his swollen face, his accent thick. Through the purpled slits over his eyes, his gaze was pleading. "It was…mistake. Didn't mean…no harm."

"He's right, Stephan," Kelly said. "Jamie's fine. It was a mistake."

Stephan glanced at Dimitri and held up his palm, then focused on Kelly once more. "If I spare Alex for you, what will you do for me, Kelly?"

Too late, she recognized the trap. Stephan knew her too well. Pride and paranoia might be his weaknesses, but sentiment was hers.

Damn! She was using her heart again instead of her

head. She really hadn't learned anything, had she? "What do you want, Stephan?"

"You think we shouldn't trust Nathan Rand. To ensure we can, I want him here where we can keep track of his movements until the shipment is safely in our hands. And since you presented the deal, I believe it would be best if you continue to be my liaison with him."

"I had only agreed to negotiate. That's all I've ever done in the past. My part in this is over. I won't participate in—"

"You have no reason to pretend squeamishness now." Stephan's gaze sharpened. "Or is there something you're not telling me about this deal?"

Kelly jammed her tongue to her teeth hard enough to stop her breath. This complication was the last thing she needed.

"Kelly?"

"No," she said. "I've told you everything."

"Excellent, then we shall proceed." Stephan flicked his hand toward Alex. "Take him back to the basement, Dimitri. Don't shoot him. Cut off his trigger finger instead."

Kelly gagged, fighting to keep her revulsion inside as the men moved away.

"I seldom give second chances, Kelly," Stephan said. He folded his handkerchief, tucked it back in his pocket and returned to sit behind his desk. "You would be wise to remember that."

Chapter 3

Kelly was good, Nathan thought, but tonight she wasn't great. Tension stiffened her shoulders and clouded her face. It was as if a curtain had come down, or a light had dimmed inside her. Although her voice was on key and her timing was perfect, she was keeping her emotions under tight control. The passion that had suffused her performance the night before was missing.

Oh, she was still sexy as hell. She couldn't help that. Just the sight of her standing in the spotlight, her eyes half-closed and her fingers wrapped around the shaft of the microphone was making Nathan's palms sweat. The dress she wore tonight was black and covered her in front to the base of her throat, but in the back it plunged enticingly to the gentle rise of her buttocks.

It was all part of the act, he suspected. This was what

Volski and the customers at his club would expect to see. Her appearance would please the crowd just as her voice would entertain them without making them uncomfortable. She packaged sex with class.

She sure had come a long way from singing in her church choir in Maple Ridge, Ohio.

He folded his arms over his chest, leaning one shoulder against the wall as he paused near the bar to watch her. He'd asked his personnel department to make some discreet inquiries into her background when he'd gone into the office this morning. What he'd learned had answered some questions, but had led to dozens more.

Kelly Elizabeth Jennings had been born twenty-six years ago, the only child of James and Cynthia Jennings. She had no criminal record and had never been arrested. How did a small-town girl, whose father ran a grocery store and whose mother gave piano lessons, get mixed up with Stephan Volski?

On the other hand, where a person started in life didn't guarantee where they would end up. Nathan was a living example of that.

The set ended to a round of applause. Kelly flashed a smile to the audience and left the stage.

Nathan pushed away from the wall and followed her through a swinging door at the rear of the club. Before he had taken three steps into the corridor, a pair of men converged on either side of him and grasped his arms.

He tensed, automatically assessing his chances. The men were probably armed like the muscle who patrolled the main room of Volski's club, but the narrow corridor would work in his favor. Their bulk was a disadvantage in close quarters. Too bad he'd given up his habit of carrying a switchblade in his boot. That would have been the easiest way to get out of this.

Had Kelly set him up? She had asked him to meet her here. If Volski hadn't agreed to their deal, he might have ordered Nathan eliminated as a security precaution.

Damn, he had no logical reason to trust Kelly, and he probably shouldn't have. After her performance the night before, both onstage and off, the only thing he was sure of was that she wasn't what she seemed. Yes, she was an enigma, an intriguing woman, but she was Volski's woman and Nathan should be cautious around her. The stakes were too high to allow room for sentiment.

Had living as Beliveau for ten years made him lose his edge?

It might be time to remind himself—and Volski's people—where he'd come from. He hadn't survived this long by being soft. Nathan flexed his arms and shifted his weight to the balls of his feet just as Kelly glanced behind her.

She stopped where she was and scowled at the men who held him. "Let him go," she said. "That's Rand. I'm expecting him."

The men were too slow to respond for Nathan's liking. He took a step forward and twisted to jerk his arms free, then gave each man a sharp nudge in the solar plexus with his elbows to discourage them from grabbing him again. He dusted off his sleeves while the men regained their breath. "You heard the lady," he said. "This dance is already taken."

The man on his left retreated fast, but his companion stood his ground, muttering something to the effect that Kelly wasn't a lady.

Nathan turned to look at him and lifted one eyebrow.

Without moving another muscle, he let the silence build from uncomfortable to threatening—a trick that he'd learned in his youth. He was only one-eighth Lakota Sioux, but he knew full well how to use his inscrutable Indian-brave look. "Sorry," he said finally. "I missed that. What did you say?"

The man's gaze wavered. "I didn't say nothin'."

Nathan decided he'd made his point. Without another word, he continued down the corridor.

The room Kelly led him to was long and narrow, with stark white walls and a clean, white tile floor. A rack of colorful dresses, each encased in a clear plastic dry-cleaner's bag, was set along one wall. Across from it, a table cluttered with various bottles and tubes sat beneath a mirror ringed with lights. Even without those clues, Nathan would have known this was Kelly's dressing room, because as soon as he followed her over the threshold, he was enveloped by her scent.

She closed the door and brushed past him. She wore her hair swept up in a rhinestone-studded clasp tonight, leaving nothing to detract from the graceful line of her bare back. Nathan had to shove his hands into the pockets of his pants so he wouldn't reach out for her.

What was it about this woman? His senses were threatening to short-circuit his brain.

"I apologize for the less than friendly reception you got back there," she said. "One of the guards at the estate had an…accident, so Stephan had to make some personnel changes. No one had a chance to tell those two who you are."

"Then I take it he wants to go forward with our deal?"

"Yes, he certainly does." She picked up the gold dress she had worn the night before from the back of a chair and gestured for him to sit. "Stephan wants to bring the shipment into O'Hare next week. Friday, to be exact. Can you have the transportation arranged and the necessary paperwork prepared by then?"

Nathan crossed one ankle over the other and leaned his shoulders against the door. *Finally!* "No problem. I'll have my end ready."

"And to make sure you do, Stephan has asked me to be your liaison."

"My liaison? What does that entail?"

"I'll be overseeing your end."

"Why?"

"Because that's the way Stephan wants it."

"Why?" he repeated.

"To ensure our mutual interests."

"In other words, your boyfriend expects you to stay chummy so you can spy on me, right?"

She draped the dress over her arm and brushed at the folds. "If I say yes, is that going to help our negotiations or hurt them?"

He smiled inwardly at her comeback. It was exactly what he had asked her the night before. He enjoyed the glimpses of Kelly's intelligence even more than the glimpses of her body.

Still, having her around was a complication he didn't need. He couldn't afford to have anyone scrutinizing his actions, especially a woman he hadn't yet figured out. Even under the best of circumstances, it wouldn't be easy to set up the sting that would deliver the drugs and Volski's gang to the feds. The clock was ticking on his debt.

Damn Tony and his bargain.

"And just how are you supposed to keep an eye on me, Kelly?" he asked. "I don't have a Mrs. Rand who would object, but from what I've heard about your boy-friend, he wouldn't look too kindly on either of us if you moved in with me. I'd prefer to keep all the body parts I was born with."

Her fingers suddenly clenched, crumpling the fabric of the dress she held into a tight ball. "I'm not respon-sible for what Stephan does."

Nathan straightened up from the door, surprised by the vehemence of her response.

"And from the way I saw you handle Stephan's watchdogs just now," she continued, "I believe you can take care of yourself, whatever happens."

It almost sounded as if she were trying to warn him. "What does that mean?"

She flexed her fingers to release her hold on the dress and tossed it back on the chair where it had been. "Where did you learn to fight like that, Nathan?" As if it was an afterthought, she moved her lips into a smile, but it didn't reach her eyes. "You moved so fast, I could hardly see it. I hope you're not that fast with every-thing. There are some things that are best done... slowly."

He regarded her curiously. She had gone into her sex-kitten mode in a bid to change the topic, but this time it wasn't working. He was far more interested in what he'd seen before she'd put on that smile. He walked past the chair to stand in front of her. "I learned how to use the particular move you saw when I was eight."

"You must have been very precocious."

"No, just resourceful. My stepfather liked little boys. I didn't let him like me."

The smile disappeared like the illusion it had been.

Her gaze clouded with horror. "My God," she murmured. "Your stepfather?"

"Well, he wasn't legally my stepfather. He never married my mother."

She touched his arm. "Oh, Nathan. I'm sorry."

"Hey, it's like you said. I learned to take care of myself."

Her hand shook against his sleeve. "Didn't your mother..." She swallowed. "She must have tried to leave, didn't she? For your sake?"

"No, she never left. I did." He covered her hand with his. "Why did you, Kelly?"

"What?"

"Why did you leave home? What made you trade the church choir in Maple Ridge for Volski's nightclub in Chicago?"

She stared at him, her lips parted in shock, then she pulled her hand away from his so fast she stumbled backward. She came up against the table beneath the mirror, knocking over several small bottles.

Nathan caught her by the shoulders to steady her, careful to keep his grip gentle. He'd wanted to take her off guard with the question—that's why he'd led up to it by giving her a piece of his past—but he hadn't anticipated this strong a reaction.

Could his gut be right? Was it possible that beneath the act she put on she was innocent?

He had to find out before she got swept up in the same net that would catch her boyfriend. He leaned down to bring his face level with hers. "Were you running from abuse the way I was, Kelly? Is that why you ended up with Volski?"

"No. My parents are wonderful. They——" She shook

her head. A lock of hair slipped loose from the rhinestone clasp and uncoiled at the nape of her neck. "How did you know about me?"

"I have connections. I asked around."

"My life is none of your business."

"I disagree. If we're going to work together, everything about you is my business."

She was struggling to draw in her emotions, but she wasn't succeeding. "You've got the wrong idea. Our relationship isn't personal, Nathan. It doesn't give you the right to ask questions like this. I realize it might have seemed as if I was leading you on last night, but—"

"No, Kelly, I knew what you were doing. It's why you're doing it that bothers me." He felt her tremble under his palms. He stroked his thumbs along her shoulders. "What's really going on? I could tell by your singing that something was troubling you tonight."

She made an odd sound in her throat. "What could possibly be troubling me?"

"If it's something to do with this heroin deal, I need to know before next week. I'm not going to work with you if you're not a hundred percent on board. Tell me now, are you a willing participant?"

"Why would you ask me that?"

"Why won't you answer?"

"Moving that heroin shipment is important to all of us, Nathan. Stephan knows he can count on me, and I intend to do everything I can to make sure it goes off precisely as planned."

Had she answered his question? He wasn't sure. "How did you get from a small town in Ohio to here?"

"I took a Greyhound."

"Were you running?"

"Yes. From boredom. If you'd been to Maple Ridge you would understand."

He touched the back of his hand to her cheek. She would have been easier to believe if he hadn't heard the note of yearning in her voice. "How did you meet Volski?"

"It's no secret." She tipped her head away from his touch. "I waited tables by day to pay my rent and sang for tips at a piano bar by night until Stephan offered me a job at this club. I took it."

"And you stay because...?"

"Because he pays me well and dresses me fabulously. It's as simple as that."

He was certain she was lying. There was far more to her story than this. He laced his fingers through the lock of hair that had come loose and cupped her nape. His gaze dropped to her mouth.

Never had he wanted to kiss a woman more than he did now. He couldn't explain it. The urge was deeper than sex and too primitive for logic. He wanted to fit his lips to hers and taste whatever truth she kept hidden, and it had nothing to do with Volski or the drugs or the debt he had to pay.

His grip tightened. He lifted his gaze to hers and saw that her eyes had darkened, the pupils expanding against a rim of vibrant green. He saw confusion...and a reflection of his own desire.

The moment stretched. It was madness to think about giving in to this attraction. He knew it, and he was sure that she did, too. Yet he leaned closer, his gaze blurring, his senses filling with her nearness, until the soft exhalation of her breath warmed his lips.

"Don't," she whispered.

He felt the word more than he heard it. "Kelly..."

She slipped her hand between them, steepled her fingers on his chest and pushed him back.

He let her do it, knowing he should be thankful, hating the fact that he wasn't.

"You still have the wrong idea," she said. "All I'm interested in from you is business, that's it. As I told you before, this isn't personal."

"If you're going to spend the next week spying on me, it's going to get damn personal."

"It doesn't have to." She slipped sideways along the dressing table until she could step clear of him. "Stephan's estate has eighty-seven acres. The main house has fifty-five rooms and there is enough guest accommodation on the property to house a small army. Unless we have business to do or you need to leave the estate, we probably won't even see each other."

"Whoa, what's this about the estate?"

"I'm not going to be moving in with you, Nathan. It's the other way around. Until the deal is done, Stephan wants you to stay with us."

The rhythm of the words was soothing, as familiar and well-worn as the rabbit Jamie clutched. Kelly pitched her voice low, savoring the peaceful hush of the evening routine. She had chosen Robert Munsch's *Love You Forever* tonight. She remembered her own mother reading it to her. They would snuggle together on the bed, just as she was doing with Jamie, only that bed had been crammed under the eaves of a bedroom a quarter the size of this one.

Kelly had liked the way the ceiling had sloped over her head. It hadn't felt cramped, it had felt cozy. In the summer, the breeze through her window had brought the sound of rustling leaves from the big maple in the front yard and the train whistle from the crossing at the bend of the highway. In the winter, she would curl up under the same quilt that her mother had used as a child, the one her grandmother had embroidered with nursery-rhyme characters.

"'I'll love you forever,'" Kelly read. "'I'll like you for always. As long as I'm living, my baby you'll be.'"

The words were a chorus that was repeated throughout the story, a song from a mother to her child. Kelly carried them in her heart. Whenever she needed to hear them, she could call up the memory of that bedroom in the house in Maple Ridge and it all came back. Not just the sounds and the images, but the feelings: safety, comfort, belonging and, above all, the persistence of love.

She brushed a kiss on the top of her son's curls before she turned the page. When she had been a child, she had listened to her mother's voice more than to the words. She hadn't understood the emotion she'd heard—it wasn't until she'd had a baby of her own that she did—yet she hadn't been too young to understand the power of a voice.

That was when Kelly had first dreamed of being a singer.

Would her mother still love her if she knew what Kelly had become?

She blinked hard to stop the rush of tears. Damn that Nathan Rand for stirring up the past with his questions yesterday. Sometimes she could go for days without thinking about it, but the home and the family she'd left behind were too much a part of her to forget for long.

She could never go back. Let her parents believe she

was still chasing her dream. They didn't know it had become a nightmare.

Yet it wasn't all a nightmare. She looked down at Jamie. Despite how he'd come into the world, she could never regret having this child. He was a gift. He was her reason for drawing breath. "'As long as I'm living,'" she whispered, "'My baby you'll be.'"

She sighed as she felt her eyes fill once more. She loved this story, but it always made her cry.

She closed the book and reached behind her to set it on the shelf above the headboard. Jamie's eyelids fluttered. He pulled his rabbit against his cheek, his lips working sleepily as his thumb inched toward his mouth. He had started dozing off a while ago, and now his body was completely lax as he lay curled on her lap, his head on her chest. He had wanted to wear his racing-car pajamas tonight, so red Ferraris decorated the flannel that covered his feet. She wrapped her hand around his toes, marveling at the miracle he was.

It was times like these that she lived for. With her child safe in her arms, the world contracted to just the two of them. He would always have her love, but there was so much more that she wanted to give him. While Stephan spent extravagantly on Jamie's material needs, there were things money couldn't buy. Jamie needed to play with children his own age. He needed a normal environment, good influences and positive role models. He deserved a future free from the taint of crime.

And in five more days…

She blotted her eyes on her sleeve and moved her gaze to the window. Through the dusk that shadowed the grounds, she could see a light in the apartment over the garage where Nathan was staying. He had surprised

her. She had assumed he would offer some resistance
to living at the estate as Stephan had suggested. Nathan
seemed astute enough to realize that Stephan's hospi-
tality was a ploy to intimidate him, yet first thing this
morning, she had heard the rumble of his motorcycle as
he'd driven through the gates.

At the sound, she hadn't been able to stop the crazy
leap of her pulse.

He was a criminal, she kept reminding herself. He
was like Stephan. He had no qualms about bringing two
tons of misery into the country.

Yes, she knew all that, yet she couldn't help feeling
there was more to him.

He'd been matter-of-fact when he'd told her about
that horror from his childhood. There had been no con-
demnation in his voice when he'd mentioned his mother,
either. From the sound of it, he'd learned to take care of
himself early on. He had intelligence, drive, and an im-
pressive insight into people. How different might his life
have been if he'd been given a better start?

And what would Stephan do to him when the heroin
he was moving went missing?

I'd prefer to keep all the body parts I was born with.
Like a cold draft on the back of her neck, the words
Nathan had spoken yesterday returned. The comment
had been half in jest, but given Stephan's track record,
Nathan had been closer to the truth than he'd realized.

Why couldn't he have been crass and rude? If he had
ogled her rather than looking her in the eye, if he had
come right out and propositioned her, wouldn't he be
easier to dismiss from her conscience?

Instead, for the past day she'd found herself haunted
by the image of an eight-year-old Nathan forced to de-

fend himself, just as she continued to be haunted by his almost-smile and that almost…kiss.

Kelly returned her gaze to Jamie. This child was her priority. For his sake, she couldn't let her resolve weaken. She would do anything for her baby.

Wouldn't she?

Nathan checked the luminous dial on his watch as he jogged past the tennis courts, careful to keep his pace steady. He was estimating the distances to various points in the estate by keeping track of how long it took him to jog it. He was also scouting out possible escape routes, but he had yet to find any way in or out other than the main gate.

For someone who was as paranoid as Volski was turning out to be, it was a good setup. The heavily wooded acreage was extremely private and enclosed by a twelve-foot-high, well-lit, electrified fence. Not only was the perimeter of the grounds patrolled by guards, the men who worked here also lived here. When they weren't on duty watching for trespassers, they kept an eye on each other. Even though the sun had set thirty minutes ago, Nathan had passed—and had been noticed by—more than half a dozen men.

The estate would be as tough to break out of as it would be to break into.

Nathan detoured around a series of terraced gardens that bordered the swimming pool and chose a path that led around the house. It was a long run, since the yellow-brick three-story building sprawled outward in two angled wings. And despite the security provided by the guards and the perimeter fence, the area between the wings was hidden behind a high stone wall

56   *Loving the Lone Wolf*

covered with ivy. What was in there? A courtyard? More gardens?

Nathan reached the front of the house and noticed that the upper floors were dark, except for the glow from a large bay window near the far end. Kelly had mentioned there were fifty-five rooms. Which one did she sleep in? Was she already in bed?

Was Volski there with her?

Something ugly and violent went through him at the thought.

I look forward to a long and profitable association with you, Mr. Rand. That's what Volski had said when he'd met him this afternoon. Although Nathan had photos of the Russian in the files he had gathered, that had been the first time he'd been face-to-face with the man he had to bring down.

Volski had been precisely what Nathan had expected. Arrogant, pretentious and coldly calculating. He'd furnished his house like a palace and had dressed himself like nobility. The thugs he'd surrounded himself with called him "sir."

Kelly had sat on the edge of Volski's desk throughout the meeting, looking beautiful and composed as she sipped tea from a gold-rimmed china cup, the perfect accessory to complete her boyfriend's image.

Nathan had been pursuing this man for more than a month. There should have been nothing in his head except the task in front of him.

Instead, his mind had been filled with Kelly.

From what he'd observed since he'd arrived here, she was Volski's girlfriend and willing partner, but Nathan couldn't picture those two together. He didn't *want* to picture those two together. When he did, it stirred feelings that were as primitive as the desire to kiss her that he felt every time he looked at her mouth.

His knuckles twinged. He glanced down and saw that he'd tightened his hands into fists. Forcing them open, he turned his back on the house and ran down the driveway. He checked his watch one last time, then slowed to a walk as he approached the long yellow-brick building that housed Stephan's fleet of cars.

The guest apartment Volski had assigned to him had been built into the space under the peak of the garage roof and as a result it was enormous, extending the full length of the building. Volski had claimed it would provide Nathan with privacy, but in reality, it did the opposite. The only way to reach the apartment was by an outside staircase, and since the staircase was in full view of the adjacent carriage house where several of the guards lived, all of Nathan's comings and goings would be observed and reported on more easily than if he'd been staying at the main house.

Nathan closed the door behind him and peeled off his T-shirt as he headed down the hall to the main bathroom. The place was decorated with overblown opulence. The floors were green marble, the picture frames were gilded with gold and the furniture was heavy and dark, with carved wooden legs and red velvet upholstery.

Nathan missed the clean, airy lines of his downtown penthouse. The furniture there was low and sleek, with nothing to detract from his view of the lake and the paintings on his walls. Yet as long as he was posing as Rand, it would be safer not to return there, anyway. Not only did staying here simplify his cover, it would allow him to gather more information about Volski's operation.

Was Volski doing the same with him? Nathan didn't

think the man's paranoia extended to electronic eaves-dropping—from what Nathan had observed, Volski's methods weren't that subtle—but just in case it did, he reasoned a bathroom would be the least likely room to be bugged. With the water of the shower running, he slipped his cell phone out of the Velcro-sealed pocket of his running shorts and thumbed in the number of Tony Monaco.

As usual, the ringing was interrupted by a series of clicks as the call was rerouted. Tony had four houses on this continent that Nathan knew of, not counting the island in the Caribbean. It was anyone's guess which place he would be using on a given day.

There was a second set of clicks before the call was finally picked up. An odd hissing noise swelled in the background. The distinctive deep voice that came through the receiver was like granite wrapped in velvet. "Talk."

He pressed the phone tighter to his ear and blocked his other ear with the heel of his hand. "Tony, it's Nathan."

"Where are you?"

"Volski's estate."

The background hissing faded. There was a muted scraping sound, like cast iron sliding across metal—a pan being taken off a stove?—then the clink of cutlery against china. "I'm assuming that is by choice," Tony said.

"More or less. He doesn't entirely trust me."

"That was to be expected." He paused briefly. When he spoke again, it sounded as if he were chewing. "You've had more than a month, Nathan."

The reminder had been spoken mildly, but that didn't diminish its impact. Tony Monaco wasn't the kind of man who needed to raise his voice to get his point across. His actions and his reputation did that for him. At one time, he had been the heir to a criminal empire that would have made Volski's operation look like a mom-and-pop corner store. Although Tony directed his energy toward other pursuits now, he hadn't come that far from his roots.

Nathan's pulse, still elevated from his run, took an extra leap. "I will pay you back, Tony."

"I hope you do. You were one of the first to join the organization, and I've enjoyed watching your success over the years. You've invested the profits from your business wisely. What are you worth now? Seventy million? Seventy-five?"

At current market value, his stock portfolio and real estate amounted to closer to eighty, not counting his art collection, but Nathan knew the exact figure was irrelevant. It wasn't money that Tony wanted.

"You've been an asset to Payback," Tony continued, "but I can't make any exceptions, even for you."

"I knew the rules going in," Nathan said. "I'm not asking for exceptions. The deal's set for this Friday."

Liquid splashed into a glass. "All right," Tony said. "What do you need?"

"A name. A contact in the FBI I can trust to bring in for the end game."

"I'll have someone get back to you on that. Which number are you using?"

Nathan recited the number for the direct line to his office at Pack Leader. He wouldn't be going back there as Beliveau until this deal was finished—he'd tied up as many loose ends as he could and had told his staff he was taking a vacation before he'd come to the estate this morning. Still, it would be safer to retrieve the message from his office voice mail there than to risk getting a call from the FBI on this phone.

But if Friday didn't go as planned, he wouldn't have an office or voice mail. He wouldn't have Pack Leader Express.

Nathan ended the call, stripped off the rest of his clothes and stepped into the shower, hoping the hot water would ease some of the knots from his muscles.

It was no use. The tension he felt was too deep for a run or a shower to loosen. In fact, it had been building for ten years, ever since the day he had joined Payback.

Payback. It was an organization as well as a philosophy. A decade ago, Tony had provided Nathan the new identity and the financial backing that had enabled him to turn his life around. Because of Tony, Nathan had given up crime. In return, Nathan had to pay back the favor by bringing another criminal to justice.

Tony had waited ten years before calling in the debt. Then two months ago, he had chosen Stephan Volski as Nathan's target. Once Volski and his heroin-smuggling ring were behind bars, Nathan's debt would be paid in full.

But if he failed to pay his debt to Tony, Nathan would lose everything that Tony's help had allowed him to build: his wealth, his company and his respectable new life.

He wouldn't just be playing Nathan Rand anymore, he would *be* him.

He would do anything to keep that from happening.

Even if it meant seeing Kelly Jennings arrested?

Nathan gritted his teeth, twisted the faucet to cold and ducked his head under the stream.

Chapter 4

The next time she had to go anywhere with Nathan, Kelly decided, they weren't going to use his motorcycle, they were going to take a car. She didn't care whether it was her own convertible or Stephan's limo or even a bus, as long as it had separate seats so she didn't have to touch him. And air-conditioning so he could wear...more.

The weather had turned sultry this morning, too hot for a jacket, so instead of thick biker leather, Nathan was wearing a plain white shirt. Whenever Kelly hung on to him, there was nothing but thin, sun-warmed cotton between her hands and the washboard ridges of his abs. She curled her fingers around the chrome loop behind the seat, trying to keep her balance as she endeavored to minimize the contact with Nathan's body.

He was a criminal—a drug smuggler—but that didn't

cancel out the fact that he was a magnificently virile man. He had the taut, well-defined muscles that came from hard use, not from bodybuilding. Each time he moved, she could feel controlled power hum through his frame.

But now that Kelly had changed position in order to hold on to the bar, she had to tighten her legs around Nathan's hips. The rumble of the engine vibrated from the soles of her feet to her thighs, setting off sparks of sexual awakening. Combined with the rubbing of his jeans against the inside of her knees whenever the bike went over a bump in the pavement, the ride was like foreplay on wheels.

Ignore it, she told herself. Think of something else.

That was the root of the problem, wasn't it? Maybe all this awareness was a subconscious way to avoid facing what she was about to do.

Kelly put her helmet close to Nathan's and raised her voice over the sound of the bike. "Turn right at the next corner. The warehouse is the last building before the road ends at the train tracks."

He nodded and slowed down to make the turn. They were passing through an industrial area southeast of the city that consisted mainly of warehouses and small plants, many of which had seen better days. The building she directed him to was no exception. Weeds sprouted along the base of the redbrick walls and decades worth of grime dulled the windows. Except for a pile of trash in the far corner, the parking lot that bordered the raised tracks beside it was empty. The only sign of recent use was the new lock that had been installed on the door.

Nathan barely waited until he had shut off the engine before he set the kickstand and slid off the bike.

He snatched off his helmet, hooked it on the handlebar and walked a few paces toward the tracks. Keeping his back to her, he shoved the tips of his fingers into the pockets of his jeans and exhaled hard. "Damn," he muttered.

She took off her own helmet, swung her leg over the seat and dismounted. "Is there a problem?"

"Yeah." Without moving his feet, he twisted to look at her over his shoulder. "But not as long as you stay over there."

One glance at him and there was no mistaking what his problem was—his body was tensed, his jaw was set in a sharp line, and his gaze was hot enough to sear her from her head to her toes.

Kelly wasn't going to pretend ignorance. The ride must have affected Nathan the same way it had affected her.

Damn, she echoed silently, biting her lip. He obviously realized as well as she did that it would be unwise to do anything about this attraction, but that didn't help. She even found his restraint sexy.

This was business, she reminded herself. He was a tool, a vital part of her plan, nothing more.

She turned back to the bike, retrieved her purse from the compartment under the seat and withdrew the key Stephan had given her. Without waiting for Nathan, she walked to the warehouse and unlocked the door.

Although it was almost noon, little sunlight penetrated the dingy windows. Pigeons fluttered near the roof, stirring up a fog of dust motes. Kelly didn't want to think about what else might be living in the dark corners. She walked briskly through the gloom to the stack of steel drums that sat in the center.

A few minutes later, Nathan's footsteps gritted across

the cement floor. His voice echoed from the cavernous interior. "What is this place?"

"It's one of Stephan's hedges against inflation. He owns a lot of real estate in the Chicago area. The taxes on this building are low enough to make it worthwhile to carry empty most of the time."

Nathan gave her plenty of space as he walked around her and headed for the drums. "You seem well-informed about his business."

"I've lived in the midst of it for three years. I haven't kept my head in the sand."

"In other words, there *is* more to you than just the packaging, isn't there, Kelly?"

This wasn't a direction she wanted to go, so she didn't reply. She couldn't afford to let the conversation get personal—Nathan had proven he was far too perceptive. He'd already expressed doubts over her commitment to this drug deal, so it was vital that she didn't do anything to increase his suspicions.

He walked along the stack of drums, occasionally rapping his knuckles against one. They all thudded hollowly. "Is it trust or mutual interest?" he asked.

"What?"

"You and Volski."

"That's none of your business. I thought we settled this already, so don't start again."

"Is that a sensitive subject?"

"It's a closed subject. Take a good look at those drums. It's what you'll be moving on Friday."

Nathan paused and rubbed the dust from the label on top of one of the drums. "Perchloroethylene? What's that?"

She was impressed by how easily he pronounced the

chemical name. Then again, Stephan was able to project an educated veneer whenever it suited him. "It's a liquid solvent that's used in dry-cleaning," she said. "It's commonly known as perc."

"And besides the real estate, Volski happens to own a chain of dry cleaners in the Chicago area, too. Boatman Cleaners, right?"

"You're well-informed yourself, Nathan."

He leaned down to study the label more carefully. "As I told you before, I have connections. I asked around. Your boyfriend has a large number of legitimate businesses such as the dry cleaners. They're why he's been able to operate under the feds' radar for so long."

Her flesh crawled at hearing Stephan referred to as her boyfriend, but it would be stupid to take issue with it. She only had to maintain the pose for a little while longer. "Don't concern yourself with the feds. Stephan always believes in insurance."

Nathan straightened up fast. For the first time since he'd entered the warehouse he looked at her directly. "Does he have someone in the FBI on his payroll? Is that what you mean?"

"Of course. It's more than his legitimate businesses that have kept him under the radar. He has friends in every law-enforcement agency that might be interested in him."

"That's good to know," he said. "I'll keep that in mind."

She regarded him curiously. He should have been relieved to hear Stephan had high-placed protection. Instead, Nathan appeared troubled.

If he only knew that the authorities were the least of his worries.

She gestured to the drums. "In addition to his property in Chicago, Stephan owns several businesses in Vladivostok, including a chemical plant. He's been importing regular shipments of perc from them for years. It's unlikely that Friday's load will get red-flagged when it comes in."

"Wouldn't cargo like this normally get transported by container ship instead of by plane?"

"Stephan alternates between both methods. He has brought it in by plane before."

"And in this case, he has customers who must be getting impatient."

"Exactly. We haven't been able to move anything since our last pipeline closed."

He grasped the top of the nearest drum, tipped it toward him and rolled it on its rim into a patch of weak sunlight to inspect it more thoroughly. "These are fifty-five-gallon drums. How many will there be?"

"Enough to fill a tractor trailer, which is precisely the same number you see here." She walked over to join him and rapped the side of the drum. "The ones that will be arriving at the airport on Friday have false bottoms that will be packed with heroin. The hidden compartments are welded into place, so they can only be accessed once the solvent has been emptied from the top. This warehouse is where we'll do it."

"Sounds good. What then?"

The pigeons fluttered overhead again. Their lilting coos sounded bizarrely calm, grating across Kelly's nerves. Until now, she had stuck to the truth, but she couldn't put this off any longer. She took a few steadying breaths to gather her courage, then launched into the lie that would change her life. "It's very simple. Once we transfer the perc from the rigged containers to these decoys, we cover our tracks by delivering the full drums from here to Stephan's dry-cleaning outlets like a normal shipment. Can your contact at Pack Leader arrange that?"

"Absolutely. And the drugs?"

"While the decoys are going out, we'll extract the heroin from the emptied drums. Most of Stephan's men will be on hand to help so it shouldn't take more than a few hours. You can start the real deliveries then."

He gripped the edge of the drum. "What about Volski? Where does he come into this?"

She brushed at some wrinkles on her pants, using the motion to dry the sweat from her palms. "With a shipment this large, he'll be here personally to supervise the unpacking and take inventory of his product. He—" She had to break off to clear her throat. "Stephan doesn't tolerate mistakes."

Nathan nodded. "So I've heard."

Her fidgeting was going to give her away, she realized. She clasped her hands together to keep them still. "As you can see, it's a sustainable plan. If this shipment works out, you and Stephan can look forward to a long and profitable association."

"That's just what he said yesterday."

"Yes, I remember."

"There's something about this you haven't told me."

There were a hundred things she hadn't told him. "If you're wondering about your percentage, Stephan will be making the arrangements to pay you."

Still holding the edge of the drum with one hand, Nathan reached out to snag her wrist with the other. "It's not about my money, Kelly, it's about you."

"I'm not part of your compensation package, Nathan."

He frowned and tugged her toward him. "Don't insult either of us by suggesting that. I'm referring to where you'll be when this deal is going down. You keep saying 'we,' but what exactly will you be doing?"

Could he feel her pulse fluttering in her wrist? She yanked at her hand. "Nathan, let go."

He pulled her to his chest and pivoted with her so that her back was to the drum. "Tell me, Kelly. Where will you be on Friday night? Are you going to be here with your boyfriend, helping him weigh his heroin?" He pressed the pad of his thumb over her pulse point. "Or are you going to be riding in the truck with me to make sure I deliver the dope to your customers?"

Neither, she thought wildly. Because that was the lie. There wouldn't be any heroin. By the time anyone realized it was missing, the entire shipment would be on its way to an incinerator.

It's the flaw of a big system. Pack Leader processes so many shipments daily that adding one more to the schedule won't make a ripple. One hand doesn't know what the other hand is doing.

Those had been Nathan's words. They were proving to be true. He had no idea that she'd already scheduled the real pickup, and from what he'd told her, he wouldn't find out.

There's an order number, but once it's in the system, there would be no reason for anyone except the client to access it.

Yes, he was the perfect scapegoat.

She tried to look past him, but his chest filled her vision. She focused on the dip at the base of his throat, her gaze centering on a vein that throbbed above the neck of his T-shirt. His heartbeat seemed to be keeping time with hers.

Would he bleed much? Would he suffer?

Or would he be fast enough to take out Stephan first?

Oh, God! How could she do this to him? How could she do it to anyone? Was living with a monster turning her into one?

Nathan lowered his voice. "Where will you be, Kelly?"

Halfway to California with her son.

Yes, she would think of Jamie. He was all that mattered.

But now that she was actually here in the warehouse, the reality of her plan was hitting home. The moment Nathan discovered the heroin was gone, he would assume he'd been cut out of the deal and he'd go after Stephan. And when the shipment didn't arrive here as scheduled, Stephan would assume Nathan had double-crossed him. The ensuing chaos would serve as a diversion, a key part of Kelly's escape plan, as was the fact that most of Stephan's men would be here with him.

Pitting the two criminals against each other didn't seem like such a good plan anymore.

"You're trembling," Nathan said. "Why?"

"Maybe it's because I'm so excited to be standing this close to you."

"Sure, that could be it." He crooked his finger beneath her chin, tipping her face upward. "Or maybe I was right and you don't really want to be a part of your boyfriend's business."

Damn him! She'd never had any trouble selling her act until he'd come along. "Stay out of this, Nathan. My relationship with Stephan is the last thing you should be concerned about."

"Believe me, I know that."

"Well, then?"

Instead of replying, he traced the edge of her jaw with his thumb. The caress was as tender—and as full of regret—as the time he'd touched her breast.

Kelly's eyes heated. His gentleness got to her. There had been so little of it in her life lately, she had almost forgotten what it was like to receive it. For an instant she wanted to blurt out the truth, to warn him to be careful, to ask him for help...

To trust her heart instead of her head?

Idiot! she told herself. She brought her hands between them and pushed at his chest. It had worked before, when they had stood like this in her dressing room, but this time he didn't move. She pushed harder.

He caught her by the waist and lifted her off the floor, holding her so that her face was level with his. "You didn't give me an answer, Kelly."

The strength she could feel in his grip left her breathless. He held her effortlessly, his arms flexed, his feet braced apart, his whole body thrumming with leashed energy.

Yet it wasn't the demonstration of physical power that held her motionless, it was the unswerving strength she saw in his gaze.

This was a man who wouldn't need trophies, she thought. He wouldn't have to barricade himself behind a twelve-foot-high fence and armed guards to feel secure. He would fight for what was his like the wolf on those delivery trucks he'd shown her, or like a proud and honorable warrior....

Where had that thought come from? she wondered.

Stress must be playing tricks with her mind. Honorable? Get real. Nathan was probably trying to play her, to use her to his advantage the same way that Stephan had. That's what men like him did. "Put me down," she said through her teeth.

"Then tell me what you'll be doing on Friday."

"Once you pick up the shipment from the airport, my part in this will be over."

"And then?"

She swallowed against the lump in her throat. "Then I'm going to sing."

He sat her down on the top of the drum and caught her face in his hands. "I'd like to hear you, Kelly."

"Nathan…"

"I mean really hear you, when you're not holding back. I'd like to see the woman you are when you're not working for Volski, the one with all the passion and the pain that you try so hard to hide."

"Stop it, Nathan. Just leave me alone."

"I can't."

"Why not?"

He moved his finger beneath her eye. It came away wet. He rubbed the moisture against his thumb. "That's why not."

Her vision blurred. Her tears were something she'd had to keep private over the past three years, just like her screams. Sentiment was a weakness, so was a conscience. She blinked hard to drive the rest of the tears away. "It's the dust."

"Uh-huh."

"We're done here."

"Not yet."

She lifted her gaze to his. It was a mistake.

She should have known the kiss was coming. It had been inevitable. The heat that had been building between the two of them from the moment they had met had been bound to reach a flash point.

Yes, she could have guessed it would happen, but she never would have guessed it would feel so...right. One second he was staring at her, his amber gaze roiling with emotions that were impossible to sort. The next instant, his lips were on hers and the world simply stopped.

His kiss was as gentle as the touch of his hands. He wasn't taking it, he was giving it. He kept his mouth supple, brushing it along her lips, stroking her slowly, thoroughly, until he found the angle where they fit best.

Then he waited.

Kelly could feel his breath, warm and easy, where the tip of his nose touched her cheek. She could sense the way his blood throbbed beneath his skin, making her own pulse grow heavy. His palms shook against her jaw where he cradled her face, but he didn't push. He'd made the first move. The next was up to her.

She closed her eyes. She was still aware enough to realize how foolhardy this was, and yet...oh, every second of his motionless caress was drawing her more surely against him.

How could this be? Why was she letting him do this, letting herself do this? She knew what he was.

Or did she?

If she made a decision, she wasn't aware of it, yet somehow she found herself sliding her tongue across his lower lip and his taste exploded through her senses.

This had to be right. Everything she had felt about him, his strength, his tenderness and his confidence, it was all here in his taste. And his mouth, oh, his lips responded to her every move, parting as she explored, stretching into a smile...

She pulled back and opened her eyes.

Yes, he was smiling. The lines at the corners of his eyes had deepened, the grooves beside his mouth had tilted and oh, Lord, were those dimples in his cheeks? He'd been handsome before, but like this, he was devastating. She lifted her hand and pressed her fingertip to one dimple.

He licked her finger and fitted his mouth back to hers. This time it was his turn to explore, and she never thought to stop him. She absorbed his taste as she learned his texture, welcoming the pressure of his tongue and his teeth. His kiss turned bolder, and pleasure shot through her body. She looped her hands behind his neck and leaned closer, giving back as good as she got.

The drum she was sitting on wobbled. Nathan wrapped his arms behind her and dragged her off, holding her suspended against him for a long, sensuous minute, letting her absorb the fit of their bodies the same way he'd shown her the fit of their mouths until she couldn't tell whether the tremors she felt were his or her own. Loosening his embrace, he let her slide down to her feet, then pushed aside her hair with his chin and kissed her neck. "Kelly?"

She thrilled to the hoarseness in his voice. In its own way, it was as much a part of their kiss as the moisture he'd left on her lips. She twisted her wrists to thrust her fingers through his hair.

"What did Volski promise you?"

At first, she couldn't make sense of his question. "What?"

He kissed her earlobe. "Whatever he's giving you, it's not enough. You don't belong with him."

The pleasure from his kiss evaporated. Reality returned with an ugly thump. Kelly tightened her grip on his hair and yanked his head up. *"What?"*

Nathan was no longer smiling. He caught her shoulders. "I know I was right. You're not happy with him. If you were, you wouldn't have kissed me like this."

She slapped his hands aside and staggered backward. Her body still throbbed, but her blood was cooling fast. She'd known kissing him was a mistake, but she hadn't realized just how big a mistake.

She wiped her mouth with the back of her hand. Her pose as Volski's girlfriend served to keep most men at a distance, yet she'd still received enough propositions over the years to recognize one when she heard it.

Had she thought this would make it easier? It didn't. It hurt. She'd hoped that Nathan was different, but she'd obviously been mistaken. When it came to her judgment in men, that was nothing new, was it?

With disbelief, she realized she was once again close to tears. "You've got the wrong idea, Nathan. I don't go to the highest bidder. I'm not for sale, so what Stephan gives me is none of your business."

In two strides he closed the distance she'd put between them, anger tightening his features. "That's not what I meant."

"I admit your kiss was a pleasant diversion, but I've had better."

"I haven't."

He couldn't mean that, she thought, steeling herself against the stupid, pathetic leap of her pulse. He was a criminal. Just like Stephan. Lying would be second nature to him.

Damn, she really hadn't learned anything, had she?

He reached for her again, but she twisted away. He closed his hands into fists and dropped them to his sides. "Kelly—"

"Unless you have some more questions about our plans for Friday, I'm going to lock up now," she said, heading for the door.

His boots pounded across the floor behind her. "Kelly, wait!"

She kept going. "We have a lot of ground to cover. Stephan wants me to make sure you get the paperwork started at Pack Leader. You said you're a relief driver, so you'll need to arrange to be working that night, too."

"Listen to me, damn it." He moved past her and stopped in front of the door, blocking her way out. "I wasn't trying to bid for you."

"Oh, I see. You wanted to sample the merchandise for free. Well, I can understand how you'd get that impression, considering how I've acted, but once again, you got the wrong idea."

"Why are you so determined to cheapen what just happened?"

"Why are you making all this fuss over a simple kiss?"

He looked at her mouth. "Do I need to show you again?"

Despite everything, her lips throbbed under his gaze. She had to fight the urge to lick them. "Don't forget why we're working together, Nathan. If we lose sight of that, we're going to screw up the deal. Is that what you want?"

"No."

"Then what *do* you want?"

He rubbed his face hard and muttered a curse.

"You said I got the wrong idea," she continued. "Here's your chance to set things straight. Why do you keep pushing me about my relationship with Stephan?"

"I'm pushing because I want to know more about you, and we don't have much time left."

"Right. We don't have much time." She waved at the space behind her. "It's Monday already. In a little over four days, there will be two tons of heroin headed for this warehouse. My priority is to make sure that everything happens according to plan. What about you?"

The heat faded from his gaze. He studied her for a minute, then looked around them, his expression hardening. "Nothing is more important to me than seeing this deal through," he said.

"Great. Then we agree on something."

"Yeah, we do." He stepped aside so that she could reach the door. "But I have one more question."

"What?"

"How the hell are we going to get back on that Harley?"

Chapter 5

If the apartment really was bugged, Nathan thought, Volski was going to think he was the cleanest man on the planet. He turned on the gold-plated taps over one of the bathroom sinks. Leaving the water running, he picked up his phone and dialed in to his office.

"Good morning. This is Pack Leader Express, Florence speaking."

Nathan's lips quirked. The advantage of having an enthusiastic executive assistant was that she worked beyond the call of duty. It was only 8:00 a.m., but he suspected Florence was already on her third cup of coffee. "Hello, Flo. You're sounding cheerful this morning."

"Oh, Mr. Beliveau! I've been here for an hour. How's your vacation going?"

"Fine, thanks."

"I'm so glad you're relaxing. It's about time. In all

the years I've worked here, I can't remember you taking a single holiday."

She was right. He didn't take holidays. Why would he? His life revolved around his business. "How's Gary doing?" he asked.

At the mention of her husband, Florence groaned. "He's the reason I got here an hour ago. It'll be another two weeks until the cast comes off and the itching is driving him crazy. He's impossible to live with."

"Sorry to hear that."

"Well, he won't be showing off on our grandson's skateboard again any time soon." She paused. "Are you at a pool already? I hear water."

Nathan looked at the sink. The drain was slow, so the water was starting to rise toward the overflow. "It's more like a fountain."

"That resort you picked sounds great."

"It's definitely a change. How are things going there, Florence?"

"The usual craziness, but nothing we can't handle. Was there anything on your voice mail that you want me to take care of?"

"I'll let you know once I check it. In the meantime, there is something I'd like you to do."

There was a rustle of paper. "Go ahead."

"I ran into an old friend down here who needs to schedule a delivery on Friday."

"Do you have the details?"

"It's a shipment of dry-cleaning chemicals coming in from Vladivostok." He was careful to keep his tone casual as he gave Florence the specifications Kelly had related to him. Although it was unusual for him to concern himself with one shipment out of the countless number Pack Leader processed each day, it wasn't without precedent. He'd done it before. It was all part of his hands-on management style. "I'd like you to make sure that gets on the schedule," he finished.

"No problem. I'll input the data right away. Anything else?"

"That's it for now."

"Maybe you should think about taking a vacation from your vacation, Mr. Beliveau. It sounds as if work is following you."

"It's why we're called Pack Leader, Florence."

She chuckled. "Enjoy the rest of your day. It's going to be another hot one in the city."

That was true. And meeting up with Kelly later wasn't going to help him cool off. Nathan terminated the connection with Florence and punched in the code to access his messages.

There were the usual invitations to fund-raisers and requests for donations to charities, but nothing that couldn't wait until next week. Finally, though, he came to the message he'd been anticipating.

"This is Derek." The man's voice was whiskey-smooth, with the trace of a Western drawl. "Tony asked me to call you with a name, but I'll be damned if I'll give it to a machine. Be in front of the Painted Pony at midnight Tuesday. I'll find you."

That was the extent of it. Nathan replayed it once to fix the voice in his memory before he erased the message.

This wasn't quite what he'd anticipated—he'd hoped to hear from the FBI directly. Still, it wasn't really surprising that Tony would go about this through an intermediary. Considering his background, Tony had to keep a low profile from the law.

All right, Nathan thought. The pieces of his plan were moving into place. The question was, could he trust whatever contact this Derek named? According to Kelly, Volski was paying off at least one federal agent. If word of this sting leaked, Nathan's life would be worthless.

Then again, he wouldn't have much of a life left if he backed out, either. Tony would make sure of that.

Nathan turned off his phone and shoved it into his pocket, then twisted the taps closed and braced his hands on the sink. He was thoughtful as he watched the water drain. Although it started slowly, the momentum built until it gathered into a whirlpool that sucked everything down with it. Just like the chain of events he was setting into motion. Once the FBI was brought in there would be no stopping what would happen.

What kind of life would Kelly have left when this was over?

She had said she would be performing on Friday and wouldn't be present when the heroin was unloaded, so there was no chance of her getting hurt in the crossfire when the sting went down. That was good. Volski's men wouldn't give up without a fight, and Nathan was glad Kelly wouldn't be anywhere near there. Yet it was unlikely she would escape the aftermath unscathed. Once the feds got their teeth into this case, Kelly would probably face charges with the rest of Volski's accomplices.

What would happen to her singing career if she ended up serving time? Would she try to turn her life around the way Nathan had, or would she look for another protector like Volski when she got out?

The more Nathan worked with Kelly, the less innocent she appeared, yet he couldn't shake the feeling he was missing a piece of the puzzle. The kiss they had shared in the warehouse yesterday had blown him away. It had been as honest as the outpouring of emotion in her voice the first night he'd heard her sing, and like her music, it had struck a chord inside him that defied logic.

It had killed him to see the hurt on her face afterward. She'd thought he was no better than Volski. Nathan had been close, damned close, to telling her the truth. He'd been tempted to warn her to be careful and to get out while she could and yet...

Right. That was a big "and yet." If he warned her, she could warn Volski. Kelly was still an enigma, and Nathan would be crazy to trust her.

And as long as Kelly thought he was Rand, she had no reason to trust him.

But he *was* Rand, deep down. Scratch away the money and the reputation he'd built as Beliveau and there was still a part of him that would always be nothing but a car thief. An unwanted bastard kid who had done whatever it took to survive on the streets.

Was that what Kelly had sensed when she'd kissed him? Maybe that's why she'd assumed the worst about him.

Yet he wanted her to assume the worst about him. His life depended on her and Volski buying his act.

Hell, could this get any more complicated?

Kelly hurried into the playroom, buttoning her blouse as she went. "Jamie?"

There was no reply. No rustle of movement, no quiet giggle or puttering raspberry noise that was his version of a car engine. Just the light padding of her bare feet on the carpet and the swish of her pulse in her ears.

She'd only let him out of her sight for a few minutes while she'd been in the shower, so he couldn't have gone far. She went to the suite's kitchen. It still smelled like the orange juice and scrambled eggs she'd fixed Jamie for breakfast. "Gloria?" she called.

There was no reply from the nanny, either. Gloria had probably decided to take Jamie to his play area in the garden early before it got too hot and had simply forgotten to tell her they were leaving the house, or maybe she hadn't wanted to disturb her in the shower.

Yes, Kelly told herself, Gloria Hahn was perfectly reliable. In fact, she was the best nanny Jamie had had yet. Although she reported to Stephan, she displayed genuine affection toward Jamie and wouldn't let him come to any harm. Kelly knew there was no reason to be so anxious. Like millions of ordinary working parents everywhere, she'd learned to handle regular separation from her child.

And yet she couldn't stop the dread that tightened her stomach. Her situation *wasn't* ordinary. What if Jamie had slipped away on his own? What if he'd found another gun? Or what if Stephan had decided to begin his...training?

Kelly raked her wet hair over her shoulders and headed for the door of the suite, unable to control the bubble of panic. The closer she got to her escape, the more difficult it was to cope with the worry. If something happened to Jamie before she got him away from here...

The chasm that opened in her heart at the mere possibility of losing her son kept her from completing the thought. She would get him away and they would find someplace safe and normal. It was only a matter of days.

A guard was lounging on the red velvet sofa in the

alcove outside the suite. He rose to his feet as she rushed through the door. One of the oblong bolsters that formed the sofa's back rolled to the floor. "You got a problem?" he asked.

She paused. "No, everything's fine. I just forgot to tell Gloria something. Do you know where she and Jamie went?"

He picked up the red bolster and pointed toward his left. "They went down the back stairs."

All right, she thought. That confirmed Jamie was with Gloria, so he would be fine. There really hadn't been any need to panic. She turned toward the staircase at the end of the corridor. "Thanks," she said.

"I heard her say something about the garage," the guard added.

The garage? Where Nathan was staying? Kelly increased her pace, a new worry forming. She had specifically asked Gloria to keep Jamie away from the garage for the rest of the week. She didn't want Nathan to find out about her son. That would give him too much leverage over her.

And considering the kiss she and Nathan had shared, she couldn't afford to give him any more pieces of the truth. He might be perceptive enough to put them together.

She hit the bottom of the stairs at a jog.

There were three guards at the door that led to the terrace. Like the guard outside her suite, they took note of her movements, but they didn't try to stop her. She had the freedom to come and go as she pleased. It was Jamie who wasn't allowed to leave the estate.

The driveway seemed endless. Heat was already rippling from the surface of the pavement as the sun beat down. By the time Kelly reached the garage, her hair

was drying but her blouse was sticking to her back. She
glanced at the staircase on the outside of the building.
There was no sign of Nathan yet. Good, she thought,
continuing to scan the area. They weren't supposed to
meet until the afternoon. Maybe she would get lucky
and he would sleep late.

She spotted Gloria's plump, dark-haired form just inside the wide opening of one of the overhead doors. At
her side, almost concealed behind the flare of her skirt,
Jamie stood holding her hand. There was a man with
them, but it wasn't Nathan—it was Alex Almari.

Kelly took a steadying breath as she approached
them. The swelling on Alex's face from the beating he'd
suffered last week had almost subsided. The scrapes
had scabbed over and the bruises were fading to shades
of yellow-green. Her gaze darted to the gauze that was
wrapped around his right hand. In spite of the bulky bandage, she could plainly see an empty space where his
index finger should have been.

Still hanging on to Jamie, Gloria laid her free hand
on Alex's sleeve. Her voice was low and urgent. "I'm so
sorry. I didn't mean to get you in trouble when I told him
about the gun. I had no idea it was you who'd left it."

"It's okay," Alex said. "Was my mistake."

"Does it…hurt?"

Alex lifted his shoulders in a stiff shrug. "Not much.
The boss gave me new job. I drive cars now."

"Wanna see my car?" Jamie asked. He held up the
tiny toy car he clutched in his fingers, innocently offering his toy to the man whose thoughtless mistake could
have cost him his life.

Alex's gaze went past the toy and focused on Kelly.
He moved his bandaged hand behind his back, as if he

were embarrassed by the evidence of his boss's displeasure. "Miss Jennings."

What could she say to him? It hadn't only been Jamie's life at risk last week. Should she comment on how she was glad Alex had only been maimed instead of murdered? How could horror be reduced to a topic for casual conversation, especially in front of a child?

Yet this was the world of her son's father. Alex would never consider thanking her for interceding on his behalf with Stephan. Brutality was the way of life here.

Kelly moved into the shade of the garage to join them. She could see that Jamie was distressed over Alex's appearance—that was probably why he'd offered Alex his car. Although she did her best to shelter Jamie, the sad fact was this wasn't the first time her son had seen one of the guards display the effects of a beating. She returned Alex's greeting, asked politely after his health, then leaned down to tousle Jamie's hair. "Hey, sweetie. You ran off without my smoochies."

Jamie puckered and gave her a noisy smack on her cheek.

Alex cleared his throat. "Miss Jennings. You need limo today?"

She shook her head, sifting her fingers through Jamie's curls. "No, I'll use something else."

"Your car?"

"No, the Navigator, I think."

Alex glanced at Gloria, then took a rag from his pocket with his good hand and mumbled an awkward goodbye. He walked to the end of the garage where Stephan's limo was parked and began to polish the car's hood.

Kelly moved her gaze to her red convertible. She'd been keeping the top up lately to reduce the chance of someone spotting the alterations she'd made to the back seat. The child-size hole she'd carved was hidden by a mohair throw…as Jamie would be when she drove him through the gate on Friday.

"I'm sorry, Miss Jennings," Gloria said, leaning her head toward Kelly's. "I know we shouldn't have gone out without telling you, but I had to apologize to Alex."

"It's all right," Kelly said, straightening up. "I understand."

"I feel as if it was my fault that he's hurt. If I hadn't said anything—"

"You had no choice, Gloria. You were only doing what was best for Jamie." Just as I am, Kelly thought.

No matter who got hurt in the process?

"We'll talk about this later," she said firmly. She did another quick scan of the area. "Right now, I'd like you to take Jamie back to the house."

Jamie climbed onto her feet and wrapped his arms around her legs, arching his back as he tipped up his chin. "Carry me, Mommy. Please, please?"

Without warning, she was seized with the familiar urge to run. It was nearly overpowering. She could actually picture herself sweeping Jamie into her arms and sprinting for the gates just the way she was, with nothing but the clothes on her back and the burning in her soul. Maybe this time by some fluke the guards wouldn't be there….

Kelly inhaled hard, fighting for control. Soon, she told herself. It was going to happen. It was. She squatted down again. "Not this time, baby. I have some business to take care of first. Will a hug do?"

He flung himself at her chest, the metal car he held digging into her shoulder. She kissed his forehead and squeezed him a little harder than she should have, only letting go when he started to squirm. She stayed where she was as Gloria led Jamie up the driveway. He didn't look back, but Kelly watched him until he was out of sight, her heart so full it felt heavy.

At times, it scared her how much she loved that child.

Seven years ago, the Painted Pony had been as classy a place as Volski's Starlight, only it had had stars on the carpet instead of the ceiling. It had featured local singers and its customers had been among Chicago's elite, but all that had changed when the man who had owned it had been convicted of kidnapping and manslaughter. Since then, it had gone through several renovations and changes in management. Currently the place was gaining popularity as a city version of a honky-tonk, and if the quality of the cars that lined the street were any indication, its latest incarnation was doing well.

Nathan spotted an empty parking space in front of a travel agency halfway up the block from the club, flipped on his turn signal and maneuvered into the spot with only inches to spare. He'd left the Harley at the estate today and was driving a black Navigator from the fleet in Volski's garage.

Using this SUV had been Kelly's idea. She hadn't offered Nathan an explanation, but she hadn't needed to. Neither of them was dancing around the fact that this physical attraction between them had to be controlled, and another torture session on his bike was the last thing they needed.

Unfortunately, the change of vehicle wasn't making much difference.

He glanced at Kelly sitting stiffly in the passenger

seat. The interior of this behemoth was big enough to carry a hockey team, yet Nathan didn't need to touch Kelly to be excruciatingly conscious of her presence.

Without the noise from the Harley, he could hear everything from her breathing to the whisper of her silk blouse and the slide of her linen pants as she shifted against the seat, reminding him about how good her body had felt when he'd held her. And with no wind whipping past them, there was nothing to stop him from enjoying the sweet, powdery scent that reached across the space between them to tease him with the memory of their kiss and the taste of her mouth.

It was torture, yes, but it was too enjoyable to end yet. He checked the time on the dashboard clock, then shut off the engine and twisted to face her. "We're a few minutes early. We'll wait here."

She looked at him. The array of lights over the entrance of the nightclub down the street shone through the windshield, etching her features with gold. "Who exactly are we waiting for, Nathan? Your explanation was a bit vague."

He tried to keep his gaze away from her mouth. He would need his brain fully functional if he was going to pull off this meeting with Derek without tipping Kelly off. He had to remember she was still reporting to Volski. "I have some loose ends to tie up."

"Are you having problems?"

"No, everything's fine. I just want to verify that the shipment of perc is on the Pack Leader schedule."

"Couldn't you just call?"

"Sure, but my company contact doesn't work for free. And he doesn't take American Express."

"So you're meeting him here to pay him."

"I'd prefer not to push my luck by going back to the Pack Leader complex. With only a few days left, I don't want to risk being spotted when I'm not supposed to be there."

"I see your point." She clasped her hands in her lap and turned her gaze back to the windshield. "We wouldn't want any complications at this stage."

"Right," he muttered. "We sure wouldn't want complications." He watched a taxi pull up to double-park in front of the Painted Pony. A group of people in jeans and cowboy boots piled out of the cab and headed for the entrance. No one appeared to look around, so he didn't think Derek was one of them. "Have you been here before, Kelly?" he asked.

"Once, a few years ago when I was looking for a job."

"I'm surprised they didn't hire you. You're a good singer."

"I was applying for a position as a waitress."

"Ah, you must have been fresh off the Greyhound from Maple Ridge."

"You got it."

"Running away from boredom."

"Yes."

"What else were you running from?"

"This question is getting boring, too."

"If you answer it, I'll stop asking."

"It's no big deal. Maple Ridge is a small town and I just wasn't comfortable there anymore."

Although she'd tossed out the comment casually, there was yearning in her voice, like the last time she'd mentioned her home. He had a crazy urge to reach across the seat and pull her into his arms, but not only would that be out of character for Rand, he suspected sympathy would make her close up. He wanted to keep her talking. "What happened, Kelly? Did you break some poor corn farmer's heart when he couldn't afford to dress you fabulously?"

Her sigh told him he'd been closer to the mark than he'd expected. "The only corn involved was the story," she said. "He wasn't a farmer, he was the boy next door. Literally."

"I hadn't realized there were any of those left."

"Believe me, they're a dying breed."

"No doubt dying of boredom."

"Oh, Marty found ways to amuse himself. While I sang in the choir and waited for him to finish med school, he went on to greener pastures."

"Greener pastures?"

"He eloped with the sister of his college room-mate and got a job at her daddy's pharmaceutical company."

Nathan didn't have to be told the rest. If Kelly had been jilted by the boy next door, that explained why she'd left home. Someone with her spirit wouldn't have tolerated Maple Ridge's pity; she would have reacted by striking out on her own. Then, in a strange city and still on the rebound, she would have been ripe for the picking when Volski had come along.

On the other hand, maybe she'd deliberately sought out a meal ticket like Volski once she'd realized she wasn't going to marry a doctor.

Nathan scowled. "Marty was obviously an idiot."

"It's a common affliction." She was silent for a while, then looked at Nathan. "Do you mind if I ask you a personal question?"

"Go ahead. Might as well even the score."

"It's about what you told me last week. That…situation with your stepfather."

He'd been half expecting her to bring this up, since he'd seen how powerfully the subject had affected her before. She must have a soft spot for children. "What about it?"

"You said you ran away. How old were you when you left?"

"Nine the first time."

"The first time? What happened?"

"Social Services took me back home. I suppose they investigated but the bastard was a slick talker. Nothing changed for long."

"Where was your real father?"

"I never knew him. He got run over by a bus before I was born."

"What about your mother? She must have known what was going on."

"Maybe on some level, but she was too afraid to rock the boat."

"Afraid? Do you mean he…beat her?"

"Only when he drank." Nathan tried to keep his tone light. Reduced to the bare facts, his childhood sounded like the plot of some cheap melodrama. "Go ahead and cue the violins."

She shifted to lean a shoulder against the door. Her hesitation was longer this time. When she did speak, her voice had softened. "Where is she now?"

"She died when I was twelve. That's when I took off for good."

"You were so young. Where did you go? How did you survive?"

"I hooked up with a gang." He patted his upper arm.

"I'd show you my tattoo, only I had it removed. Their main business was selling crack, so in exchange for food and a place to crash, I sold their dope for them."

Silence drew out. Nathan wasn't sure why he had given Kelly this particular part of the truth. Sure, telling her how he'd become a criminal helped solidify the role he was playing, but there was more to it than that. Was he trying to shock her, to widen the wedge between them?

"When we're faced with impossible choices, Nathan, there's no right answer," she murmured. "We do whatever we have to."

Or had he been hoping to see this? Compassion and sympathy, perhaps even understanding. He'd wanted another glimpse of the warmth he'd tasted in her kiss. She was an intriguing woman. "You say that as if you know about impossible choices, Kelly. What was yours?"

She studied him, her expression oddly vulnerable as her gaze searched his. She parted her lips as if she wanted to respond, but then she seemed to reconsider. The vulnerability disappeared, veiled behind the suspicious caution he was coming to know too well.

"Kelly…"

She cleared her throat and reached for the door handle. "I need some air."

He got out, went around to her side and held out his hand to help her down.

She glanced at his hand. For an instant, it seemed as if she would grasp it. Instead, she caught the handle beside the door and climbed down on her own.

"Kelly?" he repeated. "What was your choice?"

"As usual, you're making too big a deal out of some-

thing completely insignificant." She brushed at the wrinkles on the fronts of her pant legs and moved past him
to walk toward the travel agency they were parked beside. Although the place was closed for the night, she
seemed to find their window display of tourist brochures
fascinating.

"Planning a trip?" he asked.

She stiffened, then lifted one shoulder in a shrug and
moved along the window to another brochure.

Nathan swallowed his frustration at her retreat. At the
same time, he knew he should be thankful for it. How
often would he have to remind himself he couldn't afford to let Kelly distract him, especially now when they
were so close to the end?

He slammed the door and did a thorough survey of the
street, then turned his attention to the nightclub entrance
where a couple stood under the lights. They seemed familiar. He was sure he'd seen that dark, slim woman and
her red-haired companion somewhere recently….

Nathan's stomach dropped as he recognized them.
They were Clara and Phil Montgomery, the mayor's
daughter and son-in-law. Nathan had shared a table with
them last month at a thousand-dollar-a-plate Cancer
Society fund-raiser. He walked over to Kelly and caught
her arm. "We've got a problem."

She jerked at his touch. "Nathan, what—"

"Shh." He stepped in front of her so that his back was
to the Montgomerys. "See the man in front of the club?"

She stretched to look past his shoulder. "The short
redhead? The one with the tall woman?"

"Yeah." He settled his hands on her waist and eased
her toward the recessed doorway of the travel agency.
"Tell me when he's gone."

"Why? Who is he?"

"I owe him money, too." Which was true enough, Nathan thought. Phil had been one of the people who had left a message on his office voice mail. He was heading the mayor's drive to expand the city's homeless shelters and was looking for donations. "I can't pay him until next week."

"Oh."

"He thinks I'm out of town."

"He and the woman are coming this way."

Damn! This is what he got for not keeping his mind on business. He should have looked around first before he'd followed Kelly out of the Navigator. It was too late to get back inside. He brought his mouth next to Kelly's ear. "Just stay where you are and I'll do the rest."

"Nathan…"

"Where are they now?" he asked.

She moved her hands to his shoulders as she lifted onto her toes. "They're about six feet away," she whispered.

"Okay, play along." He tightened his grip on her waist and backed her against the glass door.

"What—"

He pressed his lips to hers, cutting off her protest. For the first few moments, he was almost able to tell himself he was doing this so Clara and Phil wouldn't recognize him. They wouldn't expect to see him outside a nightclub at midnight on a weekday—anyone who knew him would believe he'd more likely be at his office.

And they sure wouldn't believe Nathan Beliveau would kiss a woman on a public street. The respectable businessman they knew would be too busy overseeing his company and chasing after his next million to allow himself to be overcome by passion.

No, Beliveau wouldn't do this…but Rand would.

Nathan closed his eyes and sank into the kiss, running the tip of his tongue along the seam of Kelly's lips, coaxing her to soften, to join him.

She held herself motionless, yet he could sense her response. Through the cotton of his shirt, he felt her fingertips knead his shoulders. Her breasts nudged his chest, her nipples growing firmer with each breath she drew. He spread his fingers, sliding his hands over her hips.

Footsteps sounded from the sidewalk behind him and faded down the block. Car doors opened and closed. Four seconds later a car started up and drove off.

"They're gone," Kelly whispered against his mouth.

He cupped the back of her head and deepened the kiss, seized with a recklessness he couldn't explain. There were so many lies between them, but like his past, this was something else he could be honest about. He wanted more than her sympathy, he wanted her passion. He pressed Kelly harder against the glass door, melding his body full-length to hers, showing her without words how well they fit.

She trembled, then slid her hands down his arms, her fingers wrapping around his biceps. She tilted her head to find the angle that had worked so well the day before and kissed him back.

For a few stolen moments, the barriers between them were breached. There was no Rand, no Volski, no agenda other than a man and a woman sharing pleasure….

A car honked as it passed by on the street. A shrill whistle sounded from somewhere nearby. Kelly turned her face aside, breaking the kiss. "I said they're gone."

Nathan pressed his temple to the top of her head. "Yeah, I know."

"We can stop now."

"Can we?"

The sound she made was between a moan and a sob. "Damn you, Nathan. We have to."

Nathan knew she was right. He blinked and opened his eyes. In the glass behind Kelly, he could see a reflection of movement on the far side of the street. A tall, blond man dropped his hand from his mouth—had he been the one who had whistled?

Nathan's pulse kicked. For a second he thought the man was Dimitri Petrovich, Volski's lieutenant.

In a flash, Nathan released Kelly and spun to face the street, placing himself protectively in front of her. What the hell had he been thinking to kiss her in public? Even Rand should have known better than that.

The blond man stepped off the curb, moving into the range of a streetlight as he approached them, and Nathan's tension eased. Instead of Petrovich's pointed chin, the stranger's jaw was square. And his hair wasn't the fine, limp blond of Volski's man, it was thick and sun-streaked.

Although they had never met, Nathan knew instinctively who this had to be. The easy, loose-limbed stride, the rough-hewn features and the don't-give-a-damn tilt of the man's head were as distinctive as the whiskey-smooth drawl Nathan had heard this morning.

It appeared as if Tony's messenger had arrived right on time.

Chapter 6

Derek Stone thumped the stall door with the side of his fist. "Time's up, buddy. If it hasn't happened yet, it probably won't."

There was a scuffling and a flush. The door opened and a middle-aged man in stiff jeans and a shiny red Western shirt stepped out. "What the..." His protest trailed off as he looked from Derek to Nathan.

Apart from them, the men's room was empty. Although music from the barroom seeped through the walls, the stillness around them was total. The dripping faucet over one of the sinks echoed ominously.

Nathan assumed his inscrutable Lakota look, raised one eyebrow and tipped his head toward the men's-room door.

Without another word, the man tucked his red shirt into his jeans and hurried out.

Derek followed and swung the door shut behind him, then crossed his arms and settled his back against the door to hold it closed. Like most of the patrons of the Painted Pony, he wore jeans and a Western-style shirt, but his clothes were the real thing, faded and lived-in. He had the lanky build of a cowboy, wide-shouldered and whipcord lean. His face bore the weathered lines and deep tan of someone who spent most of his time outside.

But Nathan suspected Derek wore his easygoing cowboy manner as casually as his clothes. In spite of his drawl and the humor that played around his mouth, there was a haunted restlessness in his dark blue gaze and an air of tension in his frame. This was a man with secrets.

Yet that was to be expected. Derek Stone was a member of Payback, which meant he had a past he had chosen to leave behind. Whatever he'd done before he'd made his deal with Tony was his business. Nathan knew better than to ask.

"We have to make this fast," Derek said. "Your girlfriend didn't look too pleased about being left at the bar."

Nathan raked one hand through his hair as he leaned a hip against the edge of the nearest sink. No, Kelly hadn't been pleased about being left behind, but she hadn't put up much resistance, either. She had appeared to want some space after that kiss as much as he had. "She's not my girlfriend," he muttered. "She's Volski's."

Derek held up his palms. "You got a death wish, friend? She's easy on the eyes but that's way too dangerous for me."

"It's complicated."

"Uh-huh. I'll stick to nice simple rattlers any day."

He had a point, Nathan thought. "Tony explained what I need, right?"

"Oh, yeah." Derek's lips twitched. "Tony's got a way of expressing himself real well. When he makes you an offer, you can't refuse."

"That's Tony."

"He says you need a fed you can trust."

Nathan nodded. "Volski has someone on the inside. I have to be certain your man isn't on his payroll."

"She isn't."

"She?"

"Templar. Sandra Templar. She used to be with the Denver office but she works out of Chicago now. She's one tough old lady, and she's as straight as they come." Derek paused. "They call her The Saint."

"How do you know?"

The trace of humor faded from Derek's face. "She was my supervisor when I joined the Bureau."

Nathan felt as if he'd been blindsided. This man was a *fed?* How could Tony have let him into Payback? What had he been thinking?

Derek regarded Nathan steadily, his dark blue gaze stirring with shadows. "Relax there, chief," he drawled. "She was also the one who kicked me out."

Nathan stuck to the shade as much as he could, but sweat was already running between his shoulder blades and down his sides. The humidity had soared with sunrise, yet he had decided to go jogging anyway. This was too good an opportunity to miss.

From his apartment over the garage, he'd watched a steady exodus of vehicles first thing this morning as Volski and many of his men had left for the warehouse.

With the shipment scheduled for tomorrow, they were beginning to set up the equipment that would be needed to transfer the perc to the decoy barrels and cut open the hidden compartments that contained the heroin. Because a large percentage of Volski's personnel was involved, only a skeleton staff was left to guard the estate, giving Nathan the freedom to move around it without an audience for a change.

Nathan took the path along the electrified perimeter fence, noting only one man along the stretch where previously he'd seen three. He lifted his hand in a casual greeting. Volski's man tipped the black submachine gun he carried in return. They had become accustomed to his daily jogs. Volski had suggested more than once that he might prefer to use the workout room at the main house instead, but exercise wasn't the prime purpose of this run.

Without looking back, Nathan counted the seconds it would take him to move out of sight, then turned off the path and headed for a grove of oak trees. Pressing his back to the trunk of the largest one, he slipped his phone from the pocket of his running shorts and dialed the number Derek had given him two days ago.

There was a series of clicks before the ringing began. It was cut off by more clicks before it started again. The call was answered on the third ring. "Special Agent Templar here." The woman's voice was a feminine alto, deep and liquid, but her tone was crisp and no-nonsense. "State your business."

Nathan checked his surroundings, ready to terminate the call at the first sign of movement. "Ms. Templar, I have information about a crime that is about to take place."

"Are you calling to gloat or to confess?"

"Neither. I'm calling to hand you two tons of heroin along with the people who plan to sell it."

There was a pause, then the slam of a door and the rapid tap of heels across tile. "Who is this?" she asked. "And how did you get this number?"

"I don't plan to answer your second question, but if we reach an agreement, I'll answer your first. The drugs will be arriving in Chicago in less than forty-eight hours."

"That doesn't leave me much time."

"You won't need much time. All you have to do is show up with handcuffs. Are you interested?"

"You must already know I would be or you wouldn't have obtained this number."

"Then listen carefully. There is an informer in the Chicago bureau. It is imperative that you proceed on a need-to-know basis."

"The people on my team are clean. I make sure of it. Give me a time and a place and I'll do the rest."

There was power in this woman's voice, the confidence of an experienced commander. A tough old lady, Derek had called her. Nathan would agree with the tough part, but "old" was a relative term. Templar sounded in her forties at most, the same age as Tony.

But Nathan was no stranger to command, either. And he had a lot more riding on this than the FBI agent did. "We do this my way, Special Agent Templar," he said. "Or we don't do it at all."

"Talk. I'll listen."

"You need to assemble a strike team." Nathan paused when he saw a bush near the path by the fence sway. A sparrow emerged from the leaves and flew off. He resumed speaking. "You'll have the advantage of surprise, but you'd better prepare enough firepower to deal with between two and three dozen heavily armed men. You might also need equipment for a possible assault. The dope will be in a warehouse, approximately one hundred by one hundred-fifty feet in size, constructed of brick with four overhead doors at a loading dock on one long side and windows set under the eaves."

"That's a lot to ask on short notice. This had better be on the level."

"It is."

"If I'm going to commit that much of the Bureau's resources, I'll need more than your word. How can I trust you?"

"I understand your position," Nathan said. "But seeing as I'll be personally moving the heroin in question into that warehouse full of a few dozen armed men, I also have a problem trusting you. It's going to be my butt on the line here if you make a mistake."

"I can provide you with protection. We can discuss a deal."

"I don't need a deal. I'm merely a concerned citizen doing his civic duty. The groundwork has been laid. I've set up the trap. All I need is for you to put Stephan Volski and his accomplices in prison."

"Volski?" A muted thud sounded through the receiver, as if Templar had just sat down hard. "All right, you've got my attention. Now give me the details."

"You agree we do this my way?"

"Within reason. But before we go any further, I need to know who you are."

This was it, the point of no return. The beginning of the whirlpool. A bead of sweat seeped from Nathan's hairline to run down his forehead. He wiped it off with his wrist. Whenever he could, he avoided talking to cops. That's why he'd put this off as long as he could. Old habits died hard.

But he would have to put his faith in the authorities at some point. Otherwise, he wouldn't be able to fulfill his bargain with Tony. That was the whole philosophy of Payback. To even the score, to pay for the second chance he'd been given, he had to choose to be on the side of justice.

"My name is Nathan Beliveau...." He spoke fast, giving Templar the bare facts she would need. When he was finished, he felt drained, as if he'd already done two circuits of the estate.

Then again, he had come a long way.

He shoved his phone into his pocket, returned to the path and resumed his run just as another guard came into view. Nathan kept his face expressionless and his gait steady as he neared the main house.

Only another two days and he could go home, he thought. Once this was over, he could close the book on his past and get back to his life. Lay the ghost of Rand to rest. He could spend his days chasing yet another million and his nights wandering his office. Go to fund-raisers, give to charities and enjoy the art on his walls. And when it all got too much, climb on his Harley and open the throttle and...

"Higher! I want to go higher."

The voice was faint, high-pitched and trembling with excitement. The voice of a child. Nathan snapped his head around. He was passing the terraced gardens near the swimming pool, but there was no one in sight here, not even a guard.

"Higher!"

Nathan turned his gaze toward the back of the house. With so many hard surfaces to reflect sound, it was difficult to pinpoint which direction the voice had come from. He focused on the ivy-covered stone wall that enclosed the area between the house's two wings. He'd wondered what was behind there.

"Wheeee!"

Yes, the child was on the other side of that wall, Nathan realized. He'd already noticed a few kids on the estate—some of Volski's men lived with their families here—but those kids had been close to their teens. And why would the child of one of Volski's hired help be allowed to play at the main house?

Nathan slowed his pace as he neared the wall. It was cooler here in the shadow of the house. Along with his footsteps, he could hear a rhythmic creak. Like a swing?

"Hang on tight, sweetie."

That was Kelly's voice, Nathan realized, but he almost didn't recognize it. He'd never heard her use that tone before. It shimmered, light and pure…as if it belonged to someone from a small town who sang in a church choir and had wanted to marry the boy next door.

"More!"

"How's that?"

The child's squeal of delight mixed with a warm, musical laugh. Nathan had never heard Kelly laugh before, either, but he should have known she would sound like this. The emotion he'd heard in her singing and felt in her kiss overflowed from her laughter.

"Catch me!"

"Oof! Jamie, you rascal."

Afterward, Nathan was never able to pinpoint the moment when it all clicked. It could have been when he

first had heard the child's voice. Or the child's name—
Kelly's father's name was James. It might have been the
open warmth in Kelly's voice as she played with the boy
or the very fact that she'd done her best to keep his existence a secret. But suddenly, everything fell into place.

This was what Volski had given her. This was why
she stayed, why she worked for him, why she fought so
hard to resist the attraction that was growing between
her and Nathan. This was the key to all the contradictions he'd sensed about her.

And he'd just made the phone call that could send her
to prison.

With one more look around, Nathan changed direction and ran at the wall. He leapt to grasp the upper edge
and levered himself over the top.

He landed in sand. Plastic cracked beneath his heel.
It was a red plastic shovel that was stuck in the center
of a sandbox. The toe of his running shoe nudged a
miniature silver Jaguar. A shiny white-and-green tricycle sat in front of a rosebush covered with coral blos-
soms. Beyond that stretched an elaborate play structure
with metal climbing bars, wooden platforms and two
lemon-yellow plastic slides. From a framework painted
gaily with barber-pole stripes, a pair of swings hung on
chains. They were empty, but one of them still swayed,
the chains creaking softly.

And in front of the swings, Kelly stood clutching a
child in her arms. A child with her strawberry-blond
curls and Stephan Volski's pale blue eyes.

It was too late to run, too late to hide. One look at
Nathan's face and Kelly knew there was no point.
Jamie's parentage was obvious to anyone at one glance.

She held her son tighter, her heart pounding from the shock of Nathan's sudden appearance.

But Jamie didn't want to be held. He was twisting around, fascinated by the stranger and his unconventional arrival. Jamie was surprised by the intrusion, but he wasn't alarmed—he was accustomed to seeing all manner of tough-looking men. "Mommy, who's he?"

Nathan was dressed in running shorts and a sleeveless T-shirt, his legs and arms gleaming with a film of sweat. He stood with his feet braced apart, his muscles tensed, looking incredibly tall and astoundingly masculine, every inch a sun-bronzed warrior.

Act normal, she told herself. It was her only hope of salvaging the situation. There was no need to panic. Not yet. She couldn't let Nathan suspect this was only one part of her secret. "He's a friend of your father's, honey," she replied, shifting Jamie to her hip. "I think he must be lost."

Jamie giggled.

Nathan regarded them both in silence, his gaze snapping. Kelly could feel the force of it like a physical touch. He wasn't fooled by the casual tone she tried to project.

She felt as if she had been stripped bare, and, in a way, she had. He was staring straight at her ultimate weakness. When it came to her child, she had no defense whatsoever. Stephan knew that and exploited it all too well.

And Nathan was like Stephan. She couldn't forget that, no matter how he looked or how he kissed, no matter how her pulse continued to accelerate from his nearness.

He focused on Jamie.

Kelly couldn't help it, she took a step back. If she'd been an animal, she would have growled.

Nathan squatted to pick up one of the toy cars from the sandbox. "Hey, this is a nice one. Is it yours?"

Jamie nodded.

"A silver Jaguar," Nathan said, turning it in his fingers. "I've got one just like it at home."

"A Jag'r?" Jamie asked.

"Yeah, I like Jags." He dug another car from the sand and held it out. "Is this Hummer yours, too?"

Jamie contorted himself, trying to see. He leaned so far back from Kelly's hip that she had to put him down before he fell. "That's my yellow truck," he said, scurrying as far as his tricycle. He peered at Nathan over the handlebars. "How come you're wet?"

"Because I was running around in the sun without my hat. My name's Nathan."

"I'm Jamie."

Kelly couldn't believe what she was seeing. Not only had Nathan had the good sense to put Jamie at ease by squatting down to his level, he had managed to engage a three-year-old in conversation. No easy feat.

But Nathan was perceptive. He had a way of knowing what to say to slip past a person's guard. It would be easy for him to strike up a conversation about toy cars, too, since he would know cars. After all, he used to steal them before he started his smuggling business. He was a criminal.

A criminal with a tragic past, a childhood on the streets, an innocent victim who'd done whatever was necessary to survive....

No, she couldn't think about that. She had already let the line between them blur. Each time she saw him she came dangerously close to forgetting who and what he was. She had to rely on her brain, not her heart.

She caught Jamie before he reached the sandbox. With her hands on his shoulders, she eased his back against her legs. "This area of the house is private, Nathan," she said. "You have no business being here."

Nathan straightened up, brushed the sand off the miniature cars and moved around the roses to the tricycle. He handed the cars to Jamie, then lifted his gaze to hers. "Kelly, we need to talk."

The turmoil in his eyes took her by surprise. What did *he* have to be upset about? She squeezed Jamie's shoulders. "There's nothing to discuss. We don't—"

"Miss Jennings!"

At the call, Kelly looked behind her.

Gloria Hahn hurried through the terrace doors that stood open to the house, her clothes awry and her dark hair loose around her shoulders. "I'm sorry I slept in," Gloria said, clearly out of breath.

Kelly winced. She'd slipped a dose of sleeping pills into Gloria's evening cup of tea last night as a trial run. She'd needed to check how effective they would be—she couldn't have Gloria awake to report Jamie's absence to Stephan on Friday. "Don't apologize, Gloria," she said. "It's not your fault."

"Please don't tell Mr. Volski. I didn't hear my alarm…" Her apology wound down in midsentence when she caught sight of Nathan. She frowned and looked at Kelly. "Do you want me to call Dimitri? He didn't go with the rest."

"No, Gloria," Kelly said. "That won't be necessary. Mr. Rand was just leaving."

Nathan glanced at the house, then looked at Kelly and lowered his voice. "Send her away."

"Nathan—"

"I don't think you want anyone else to hear what I have to say."

Something in his tone alerted her. It wasn't exactly a threat. It didn't have to be. Neither of them wanted what passed between them getting back to Stephan. Kelly bent down to give Jamie a hug, then turned him around and nudged him toward Gloria. "Those cookies we made should be cool enough to eat now, sweetie. Want to give them a try?"

Jamie twisted his head to look up at her, the cars Nathan had returned to him clutched in each fist. "I want to play cars."

"We'll make a garage with the cushions again, okay?" She smiled and dropped a kiss on his curls. "Go with Gloria. I'll be right there."

Nathan barely waited until the terrace doors had closed behind Gloria and Jamie before he grasped Kelly's arm. He guided her around the swing set to a marble slab bench nestled at the base of the wall that enclosed the yard. "Why didn't you tell me?" he demanded.

There was no point pretending she didn't know what he meant. "My son is none of your business."

"Wrong." He waited until she sat, then straddled the bench beside her. "I told you before, everything about you is my business. I needed to know if you're a willing participant in our heroin deal. Your son just gave me the answer."

"Jamie has nothing to do with our deal."

"He's the reason you're here, isn't he?" Nathan lifted his hand as if he was about to touch her again, then glanced at the house and flattened his palm on the marble between them. "It makes sense now. All the passion and rage the first night I heard you sing, it was because of your son."

"It was because I'm paid to sing. That's what I do. Why is it so hard for you to accept that?"

"Because I felt the truth both times you kissed me, but you were so full of contradictions, I hadn't figured it out until now. Your child is the reason you're staying with Volski and doing his bidding."

"I wouldn't put it like that. You have a bad habit of making a big deal out of noth—"

"Kelly, stop. It's too late. I saw your love for Jamie. I heard it. That child is more than a big deal, he's the center of your life and he changes everything." He spread his fingers on the marble a breath away from her hip. "Is Volski threatening you?"

"What?"

"If he is, you do have a choice. You don't have to stay."

"Nathan…"

"Sometimes women remain in a relationship where they're not happy because they're afraid of what will happen if they leave. You're a good singer. You're talented enough to make it without his support."

It almost sounded as if he'd guessed what she planned for tomorrow… No. It wasn't possible. He was perceptive, yes, but he couldn't be a mind reader. She fought for composure. "Nathan, keep out of this."

"Kelly, I know what I'm talking about." He locked his elbow straight and leaned closer. "I saw the pattern with my mother. She kept turning a blind eye to what my stepfather was like because she believed she didn't have the means to support us on her own."

This had to be the source of his turmoil, she realized. It must be why he looked so intense. Despite the path he had chosen as an adult, he would still be haunted by what he had endured as a child. "I'm sorry for what you went through, Nathan, but—"

"This isn't about me, it's about you."

"My circumstances are completely different from what you experienced when you were growing up. Stephan doesn't abuse me, and he would never hurt Jamie. He goes out of his way to protect him."

"It isn't only physical abuse that leaves scars on a child. Is this really how you want to raise your son?"

His words ripped straight to her heart. No, she had no defenses where her son was concerned. Tears choked her throat. "You have no right to judge me."

"I'm not judging you. That's the last thing I would do." He shifted, bringing his knee against the side of her leg. "And if I could, I wouldn't push you like this but there isn't much time. Kelly, let me help you."

Yes! she wanted to scream. Oh, yes, for the love of God, please help me. I've been so alone for so long....

She was close to telling him everything. He looked so strong and competent, sitting here in front of her with his broad shoulders bared by that sleeveless T-shirt and his arms flexed as if he were seconds away from holding her. Compassion swirled in his amber gaze, protectiveness hardened his jaw.

Yet he was already helping her, she thought. He would play a vital, if unwitting, role in her escape.

Oh, God! The nearer it got, the less she wanted to go through with her plan. Actually allowing the drugs to be delivered was unthinkable, but she didn't want to betray Nathan. She longed for another way out, yet could she trust this man whom she'd known for less than a week to rescue her like some fairy-tale hero?

A hero who had a flat scar on his upper arm where he used to have a gang tattoo.

A man on the wrong side of the law, part of the very world she wanted to escape.

A criminal who was Stephan's business partner, who had no qualms about smuggling two tons of heroin and could even now be thinking of some way to use this weakness of hers to his advantage.

Was she an idiot?

She pressed her fingertips to her temples. Think, *think!* "Hypothetically speaking, what kind of help are you offering, Nathan?"

"I'll make sure you and your son are taken care of."

"Taken care of?" she repeated. "Is this a roundabout way of topping Stephan's bid? Would you expect me to repay your favor by giving you mine?"

"Damn it, Kelly, I already told you that's not what I want." His knee nudged more firmly against her leg. "Sure, I'd like to kiss you again. I'd like to do a hell of a lot more than kiss you, but I'm not that much of a bastard. I would want you willing, not bought."

She looked at his knee, her nerves jumping, then slid her gaze to his muscular thigh. They were in broad daylight, in view of anyone who happened to be at the back of the house. His words weren't tender or gentle, yet a thrill shot through her at his bold declaration. What on earth was wrong with her?

"I'll find you another job," he said. "That's what I meant. I have connections, and I have the resources to help you establish a new life with your son. You'd be surprised by what I can do for you."

"What about Stephan?" She twined her fingers together in her lap, hoping he wouldn't see how her hands shook, but the trembling spread to her arms. She wanted so much to be able to believe…yet she would be gambling her son's future if she did. There wouldn't be a second chance. The last time she'd trusted a man, she'd been completely, horribly wrong. "What about your deal with him?"

"That's a separate situation."

"Really?" she asked. "It's why you're here, isn't it?"

"Yes."

"You don't want to mess up your plans to bring in the shipment, do you?"

"Hell, no. I've got too much riding on it now. The deal has to go through."

There was no mistaking the ring of conviction in his voice. Kelly didn't doubt he meant what he said. About that, anyway. "Still speaking hypothetically then, do you think Stephan will let you touch his heroin if you interfere with me and his son?"

"Kelly—"

"Do you think I'm fool enough to believe that Nathan Rand would choose sentiment over profit?"

His jaw twitched. Gradually, his expression shuttered. "I'm talking about afterward, Kelly. As long as you're willing, I can help you when the deal's over, but you have to separate yourself from Stephan now."

"I see. And what about your future deals, your long and profitable association with Stephan's organization? Do you expect me to believe you're prepared to throw that away for someone you've just met?"

"Kelly, I understand that you'd be skeptical about my motives, but—"

"*Skeptical* doesn't even come close to describing how I feel." She took a deep breath. "This doesn't add up. You're too smart not to realize the consequences of what you're offering me. What's your real agenda? Why do you want to separate me from Stephan?"

He rose to his feet. "It's for your own good, Kelly. You'll just have to trust me."

"Trust you, Nathan?" She tipped up her chin to look at him, her eyes burning. "Can you give me one good reason why I should?"

He didn't reply.

Please, she thought. Just one good reason so I won't have to go through with my plan. Tell me something that would make me believe in fairy tales and prove my heart is right about what I feel when you touch me.

And she wanted him to touch her again. She longed to feel his arms around her, press her body to his and find the perfect fit of their mouths. She didn't have any doubts when she kissed him. Then they were simply a man and a woman, sharing a bond that defied logic.

He stared at her for a full minute, his face hard with strain. "I'm sorry, Kelly," he said finally. "I can't do that."

She felt a twinge of pain as her nails bit into her palms. "Nathan, how can I trust you if you don't trust me?"

He had no answer to that one. He shook his head once and glanced around the yard.

Kelly wiped her eyes with her knuckles and stood. "It's on the other side of the rosebush."

"What is?"

"The way out. That's what you're looking for, isn't it?"

Chapter 7

"Join me," Stephan said, his aristocratic features smoothing into a smile as he moved to stand beside the fireplace. He picked up one of the crystal shot glasses from the silver tray Alex offered and motioned him to serve the others. "I wish to propose a toast."

Alex glanced around Stephan's office, as if uncertain whom to serve next, then crossed the carpet to where Nathan stood by the velvet drapes that flanked the French doors. He waited until Nathan had taken a glass from the tray, then walked over to Kelly.

Someone had changed Alex's bandage—it was less bulky now—yet he still wasn't using his right hand. He held the tray awkwardly in his left, his features pinched with concentration as he endeavored to keep it steady. His new duties as one of the drivers wouldn't include serving drinks at the main house. Kelly knew that Stephan had brought him here to make a point.

I seldom give second chances, Kelly. You would be wise to remember that.

It had been almost a week since Stephan had said those words. He'd meant them for her. Kelly hadn't forgotten, but the threat also applied to Nathan.

"Kelly, my dear. You're keeping us waiting."

She arranged her face into a smile and slid off the desk. "That's a woman's prerogative," she said, picking up a glass. She didn't like vodka any more than she liked Stephan's Russian tea. She was getting far too good at doing what she didn't like.

Alex set the empty tray on the table that held the samovar. At Stephan's nod, he left the room, closing the door behind him.

"I thought it was changing her mind that was a woman's prerogative," Stephan commented.

Changing her mind? That was exactly what had plagued her all day. Somehow Kelly kept her smile in place. "You're right, of course," she said. "I changed my mind about not having a drink. What are we toasting?"

"Success." Stephan walked toward Nathan. "Everything is falling into place. By this time tomorrow, we will have accomplished a coup that will immortalize us both as businessmen without equal."

Nathan rotated his glass in the light, studying the swirling design on the crystal. "I couldn't agree more, Stephan. What will happen tomorrow will be the stuff of legend."

"This shipment is only the beginning," Stephan said. "We currently serve customers from the Genero family in both New York and Atlanta to the Canyon Brotherhood in South Dakota, but with your transportation and my superior product, by next year at this time I envision a distribution network that spans the entire nation."

Kelly tried to tune Stephan out as he continued with his long-winded toast. She had been instrumental in setting up the deals with many of his current customers, and she felt guilty for playing even the smallest role in this obscene business. The Atlanta Generos were vicious pushers. The militia group in South Dakota that called itself the Canyon Brotherhood was rumored to have ties to terrorists. Yet following Stephan's orders had been the only way she could continue to see Jamie, so she'd believed that she'd had no choice.

But within twenty-four hours, all of that would be over. Yes, by this time tomorrow, she would have accomplished a coup of her own.

Stephan finally finished his toast and raised his glass with a flourish. "To the future!"

"Yes. To the future," Nathan echoed. He lifted his glass and looked at Kelly. Something sharp stirred in his amber gaze. "May we all get what we want."

Kelly's pulse tripped. She had the feeling that he'd meant that last sentence for her.

Since that emotional scene in the garden this morning, he had limited their conversations to business. He'd been scrupulous about not touching her, and he hadn't renewed his offer to help her.

Yet something between them had shifted, as if a chink had developed in the wall he kept over his feelings. More and more, she caught glimpses of anxiety on his face.

Was he worried about her?

Or was he worried she was going to tell Stephan what he'd offered?

She had been too distraught to think clearly at the time. It was only later that she had understood the power

Nathan had handed her. With one word to Stephan, she could denounce him as untrustworthy and reveal how he'd been plotting to take away two of his partner's prize possessions. He probably realized that she could scuttle his hopes of seeing any profit from the drugs he planned to smuggle.

She had said that she couldn't trust him unless he trusted her, yet in a way, by approaching her at all, he *had* trusted her.

And that was why she'd been plagued with thoughts about changing her mind.

Crystal clinked on crystal as Stephan touched the rim of his glass to Nathan's. He tossed back his drink in one gulp.

Nathan took a sip and regarded his glass.

"It is the custom in Russia," Stephan said. "When we drink a toast, we must drain the glass."

Nathan shrugged his shoulders and took another sip. "I've never seen much point in that. I prefer to savor my pleasures."

Annoyance tightened Stephan's lips—Kelly knew he hated being contradicted—but he quickly covered the reaction with a hospitable smile. "Then tell me about the customs of your people, Nathan."

Nathan lifted an eyebrow. "Americans?"

Stephan used his free hand to make a gesture that encompassed Nathan's face and hair. "I meant your tribe. It is obvious that you have some Indian blood."

Kelly held her breath, waiting for Nathan's reaction.

But if Stephan had been trying to provoke him, it didn't work. Nathan kept his tone level and his expression impassive as he replied. "My great-grandfather was a Lakota Sioux. I don't know what his toasting preferences were, but I heard his people were quite good with knives."

Stephan regarded him in silence, as if trying to decide whether the words had been meant as a threat.

Nathan glanced at Kelly. "But I don't put too much stock in heredity. I believe it's how we use what we're born with that matters."

Oh, she hoped that was true. She hated to think of what Jamie might have inherited from his father. "I suppose," she said.

Stephan retrieved the vodka bottle and refilled his glass. "We were toasting our future success," he said. "It is a subject worthy of another round."

A second long-winded toast followed. While Stephan's words droned around her, Kelly took the time to study him and his business partner.

The physical differences between the two men were striking. In addition to the contrast in their coloring, Stephan was a head shorter than Nathan and was likely thirty pounds lighter. Stephan wore an obscenely expensive suit of gray silk and a perfectly knotted tie, the picture of elegance. Nathan wore his customary white dress shirt with the collar open and the sleeves rolled up, black jeans and motorcycle boots. He didn't look elegant—he looked rough-edged and sexy.

As far as body language went, Stephan held himself stiffly with the out-thrust chest and protruding chin of a bully. Nathan stood with the watchful, easy confidence of a wolf.

There were more differences that weren't readily visible. Stephan was cunning while Nathan was thoughtful. Stephan manipulated through fear while Nathan used insight. And in three years, Kelly had never seen Stephan take the time to squat down to his son's level and strike up a friendly conversation about something Jamie was interested in.

Stephan's visits with his child were brief and formal. He regarded Jamie as a possession, not a person. As a result, Jamie had never warmed to his father, even though he was an otherwise friendly child.

Yet Jamie had responded instantly to Nathan.

Of course. With the instincts of a child, her son had sensed that the two men were not the same. Inside, Stephan was a monster. Nathan wasn't.

And there was no way on earth that Kelly could go through with her plan to double-cross Nathan and leave him to Stephan's mercy.

"Are you not joining us in our toast, Kelly?" Stephan asked.

She downed what was left of her drink, hoping Stephan would assume it was the strong liquor that made her eyes water. She blinked to clear her gaze, glancing from one man to the other.

Granted, Nathan was a criminal. That was the one aspect he did share with Stephan, but if Kelly was going to condemn him only on the basis of how he earned a living, she might as well condemn herself.

She still didn't trust him...but she didn't have to trust him to save him, did she?

The wave of relief that followed that realization was so strong, she staggered. She covered it with a low chuckle as she placed her glass on the desk. "That's enough for me," she said. "I'll say good night."

To her surprise, Stephan didn't try to stop her from leaving. Usually he liked his ornament to remain until the end of any meeting.

But Kelly didn't pause to analyze his behavior. She was able to look Nathan in the eye before she left and it felt good. Maybe the next time she glanced in a mirror, she'd be able to look herself in the eye, too.

Her steps grew lighter as she neared her suite. For the first time, there was no guard on the sofa outside the door. Many had been pulled from their duty at the house to patrol the warehouse in preparation for tomorrow. The easing of security was what she was counting on, yet now she could regard it with a clear conscience.

She was still going to take this opportunity to leave with Jamie—she couldn't conceive of anything that would make her stay. But once the heroin was on the way to the incinerator and she and Jamie were on their way to freedom, there was no reason why she couldn't call Nathan and warn him what she'd done.

Yes! she thought, the solution was becoming clearer by the second. All it would take would be one phone call. If Nathan learned that she alone was responsible for the missing heroin, he wouldn't have any reason to confront Stephan. Sure, Nathan would be furious with her, but at least he would have a fighting chance of avoiding Stephan's wrath.

It was a risk. If Nathan was angry enough to come after her, or worse, if he went to Stephan with what she told him, she and Jamie would be losing most of their head start.

But setting Nathan up as a scapegoat was no longer an option. It never had been. She'd been deluding herself to think she could do that to anyone.

She slipped into the suite, surprised to see that the sitting room was dark. Gloria liked to watch Letterman while she was waiting for Kelly to return. Had she fallen asleep already? Was this an aftereffect of the sleeping pills Kelly had given her yesterday? She switched on a light and saw at a glance she was the only one here. No, not quite. Jamie's rabbit lay discarded in the center of the floor.

She scooped up the rabbit and walked toward Jamie's bedroom. It was odd that Gloria would have put Jamie to bed without his favorite toy. "Gloria?" she called softly. "I'm back."

There was no reply. No rustle of bedclothes, no creak of the rocking chair across from the bed, no sleepy demand from Jamie for his bunny. The bedroom was dark, too. Jamie never slept without a nightlight.

Even before she crossed the threshold of Jamie's room, the dread was starting to build. It began in the pit of her stomach, a cold knot of emptiness that she didn't want to acknowledge, didn't want to admit was real. She slapped her palm against the light switch on the wall.

The bed was empty. The covers were neatly smoothed, but the rest of the room wasn't neat. The drawers that held Jamie's clothes were open, the garments that had been folded inside were rumpled into piles or spilled in heaps on the floor. The closet door stood ajar. There were empty hangers and gaps in the neat row of tiny shoes that lined the shelf in the bottom.

She had been waiting until the last minute to pack his things.

It looked as if someone had beaten her to it.

"No," Kelly breathed. "Oh, God. No. Jamie?" She pivoted and raced through the rest of the suite, switching on lights as she went, trying to outrun the dread before it congealed to certainty. "Jamie? Jamie, where are you? Answer me, baby!"

Jamie had been fine when she'd left for the Starlight after dinner. She'd done two sets tonight, and then had been delayed by that meeting with Stephan and Nathan, but she hadn't been gone all that long. If he'd been hurt or fallen ill, Gloria would have phoned her. Stephan would have known, too. He was always alerted when it concerned Jamie's welfare.

And if there had been a medical emergency, no one would have taken the time to go through Jamie's room and pack his clothes.

She hadn't realized she was crying until she tasted the salt as her tears ran into her mouth. She stopped in the center of the playroom and wiped her cheeks on the rabbit she still clutched, then pressed the toy to her nose. It carried a trace of Jamie's scent, the sweet mixture of baby shampoo and little boy.

This was different from the panic she'd felt before. This wasn't a false alarm, it wasn't due to a misunderstanding or a failure in communication or any of those innocent explanations that would end in a laugh of relief as she ruffled Jamie's hair and asked him for her smoochies.

She knew, deep in her gut with a mother's instinct. She *knew*.

Her baby was gone. Someone had taken him.

Someone?

"My goodness, Kelly. It appears you have no head for vodka. Are those tears?"

At Stephan's voice, she whirled to face the door. "Where is he?"

Stephan stepped into the playroom and moved his gaze along the shelves of toys, his expression smug. "My son is being well cared for. There's no need for the dramatics."

She tossed the rabbit onto the bare couch—the cushions were still leaning together on the floor for a garage. "Where is he?" she repeated.

"He's in a safe place." He snickered. "A very safe place."

It was the nightmare that had lurked in the back of her mind for three years. It was why she had been so desperate to leave now, before it was too late.

But it *was* too late.

She rounded the cushion-garage and walked to Stephan, trembling as her dread flipped over to rage. "You can't do this."

"Kelly, we both know that I can do whatever I want. The child is mine. I have the medical tests that prove it, and as I've told you before, I am prepared to use them."

A crimson haze fell over her vision. Something fierce and primal stirred in her heart. She caught Stephan by the lapels of his suit, fisting her hands so tightly she could hear stitches pop.

She wanted to shake him. She wanted to kill him. He had taken her baby. She brought her face to his. "You son of a bitch. Jamie is *mine.*"

Eyes the same pale blue as Jamie's stared back at her. "Take your hands off me."

She heard the warning in his tone but she was too far gone to heed it. "Bring him back. Now."

He struck her wrists, knocking her hands aside.

Pain shot up her arms. The crimson haze thickened, obscuring three years of restraint. He had taken her baby, her reason for living. She had nothing left to lose. She curled her fingers into claws and lunged for his face.

She had the satisfaction of feeling her nails sink into

flesh before her arms were seized from behind. She was yanked backward so hard, her jaw snapped shut.

"I'm sorry, Mr. Volski," Dimitri said. He jerked Kelly another step back, dragging her heels across the carpet. "She moved too fast."

Kelly hadn't even noticed that Dimitri had come into the room. She threw her weight forward and stomped her heel on his foot.

Dimitri's thumbs dug into the soft flesh of her upper arms hard enough to make her cry out. "Be still," he ordered.

The pain triggered a fresh wave of tears. Kelly blinked hard, focusing on Stephan.

His face was flushed, the shade of red deep enough to verge on purple except for the pinched white rim around his mouth. Droplets of blood welled in four ragged parallel lines down his left cheek.

She had made him bleed. Kelly knew she should be horrified by what she had done. Part of her was. But most of her wanted to do more. She flexed her fingers, aching with her helplessness. "You don't love him," she said. Her voice was so raw, her throat hurt. "You don't care about him. He needs me."

Stephan pulled his handkerchief from the breast pocket of his suit and pressed it to his scored cheek. "I don't believe you understand your position here, Kelly."

"Is Gloria with him?"

"That is no longer your concern."

"Of course, Gloria must be with him. She's not here, and none of your men would know how to take care of a child. But he left his rabbit behind. He can't sleep without that toy. You have to—"

"Silence!" Stephan stepped forward and backhanded her across the jaw. "You try my patience."

Kelly tasted blood where the inside of her cheek hit her teeth. It helped sober her. So did the throbbing in her wrists and her arms and her jaw. It made her realize how precarious her position was. Stephan could order Dimitri to take her outside and shoot her. She would disappear, just like so many people who had opposed Stephan over the years.

She might have nothing left to lose, but Jamie did. She was his only hope.

Oh, dear God! The nightmare kept getting worse. If something happened to her, what would become of her son? Would he grow up to be like Stephan?

Or would he grow up to run away, to live on the streets, join a gang, traffic in drugs and steal cars the way Nathan had....

A sob tore from her throat. She had to lock her knees to keep herself from collapsing in Dimitri's grip.

"The child lacks for nothing," Stephan said. He took the handkerchief from his cheek and looked at the bright red lines on the linen. Fury coiled in his gaze. He refolded the cloth to a fresh side and pressed it back to his face. "And as I said, that is not your concern."

I'm his mother, you unfeeling bastard. It's my only concern!

Somehow she kept the words inside. Antagonizing Stephan further wasn't going to help Jamie. "What do you want from me, Stephan?"

"Ah. That's better. I see you do understand."

"I'm already working for you. What else do you want?"

"I want to ensure my heroin comes in on schedule. All of it."

He couldn't know, she told herself. He couldn't. This was just his paranoia. "That's what Rand and I have been doing all week."

"Oh, you and Rand have been doing more than that, Kelly. It's come to my attention that you two are becoming rather friendly."

"You told me to be your liaison with him."

"I don't care if you're going on your back five times a day for him as long as you're discreet. I no longer have any interest in using you that way. That's not the issue. I simply want to make sure I get my shipment."

His crudeness disgusted her. How could she ever have let this monster touch her? But as he said, that wasn't the issue. It was his money that he cared about, his dope, his deal that would make history.

The pieces fell into place with a sickening certainty. "You're using Jamie as a pawn. You're holding him hostage so that I make certain Rand follows through."

"I prefer to think of it as insurance."

"And once you have the shipment, will you bring Jamie back to me?"

"Of course, Kelly. Tomorrow. After it's done."

"There are only two and a half hours to go before the flight lands, Mr. Beliveau," Templar said, her suspicion crackling through the phone. "You can't open negotiations now. What kind of scam are you trying to pull?"

"No scam," Nathan said. "As I told you before, we either do this my way or not at all."

"Will she cooperate?"

"Yes."

"I'll see what I can do."

"That's not good enough. I want you to give me your word now."

"Mr. Beliveau—"

"Agent Templar, you guarantee that Kelly Jennings gets immunity and you put her and her son in the witness protection program or nothing happens."

"Fine."

Nathan shoved his phone into the pocket of his jeans and blew out the breath he'd been holding. Templar had bought his bluff.

Except he wasn't sure it had been a bluff.

He rubbed his face, then slammed out of the bathroom, grabbed his helmet and left the apartment.

The sticky air hit him like a wall as soon as he stepped onto the landing at the top of the staircase. The mass of humidity that had stalled over the Chicago area at the beginning of the week had reached its saturation point, making it difficult to breathe. Through the boughs of the trees that lined the driveway, Nathan caught glimpses of heat lightning strobing through the clouds. There was going to be a storm tonight. He could feel it.

Damn. The landing schedule at O'Hare was chronically overcrowded. A thunderstorm would stack up the entire queue. That's all he needed. Another complication.

One way or another, this deal had to go through. He could only hope if the cargo flight was delayed or rerouted, it wouldn't negate the immunity he'd worked out for Kelly.

He was taking it on faith that Kelly would cooperate with the FBI. The way she'd looked when she'd held her son yesterday, with that fearsome protectiveness glowing from her face, had convinced him she would do whatever was best for that child.

But if he'd read the situation wrong and she had reported their conversation to Volski, Nathan could be dead by the end of the night.

Complicated? Hell, this was getting downright dangerous. He returned to the apartment and dug his rain slicker out of his duffel bag, then clattered down the stairs.

"Hello, Nathan."

He was surprised to hear Kelly's voice. He hopped from the last step and turned so he could look in the shadows under the staircase where he'd left his bike.

She was sitting sideways on the seat, a spare helmet propped on the gas tank beside her. The floodlight that was mounted on the side of the garage shone through the steps, casting wide bars on her face. Her silk blouse gleamed palely in the alternating shadows, covering her arms to the wrists but baring her throat and the first hint of her cleavage.

As always, the sight of her made his blood pump a bit harder. He moved around the base of the stairs. "What are you doing here, Kelly?"

"Waiting for you."

He walked to the bike and rested one hand on the end of the handlebars. This was the last thing he'd expected. He'd counted on her being safely out of the line of fire. "Why aren't you at the club? You said you'd be performing."

She wore her hair loose tonight. It fell over the left side of her face, her curls tinged copper where the floodlight hit them. "There has been a change of plans," she said. "The show was canceled. I'm coming along with you."

"You can't."

"Stephan's orders. I'll be sticking right with you until his heroin has been delivered into his hands."

"Not possible. I won't be able to explain your presence at the terminal."

"You appeared to know your way around pretty well when you took me there a week ago. I'm sure a smart guy like you will think of something."

Her voice had a brittle quality that made him uneasy. She was trying to be tough, but she couldn't pull it off. He moved closer, noticing her eyes seemed too bright. "What's wrong, Kelly?"

"I'm just seeing to our mutual interests, Nathan."

"We'll have to take my bike."

"That's why I borrowed this helmet again."

"It's going to rain."

"I won't melt."

No, but judging by the way she held herself, she looked as if she was strung so tight she might shatter. Nathan hung his slicker and his helmet from the end of the handlebars and lifted his hand toward Kelly.

She jerked back before he could touch her, moving so fast she lost her balance. He caught her by the arms before she could slide off the seat. "Kelly…"

She clenched her jaw, inhaling sharply through her nose. The sheen in her eyes grew brighter. "Let go of me," she bit out.

He released her immediately, startled by her vehemence. "I was only trying to help."

She made a sound that he wouldn't call a laugh. He'd heard her laugh yesterday morning, and those warm, musical tones had been nothing like this. "Too late, Nathan," she said. She picked up the spare helmet. "Shall we go?"

He studied her, trying to get a read on her distress. Was she having second thoughts about staying with Volski? Did she think it was too late to change her mind?

She pushed her hair behind her ears and lifted the helmet. A bar of light fell across her jaw, yet there was still a shadow there, a dark, purple smear that looked like...a bruise.

Nathan sucked in his breath. He grabbed the helmet from her hands. "Did Volski do that?"

"What?"

He put his index finger under her chin and focused on her injury. The fury that went through him was so strong, it took every ounce of his restraint to keep his touch gentle. "He hit you."

She gave another one of those sounds that was too bitter to be a laugh. "Believe it or not, it was the first time he has. He made it count."

Nathan lifted a strand of hair from her cheek and tucked it behind her ear. "Oh, Kelly, I'm sorry."

"Why? I take it you haven't talked to the bastard today or you would have seen what I did to him."

"Kelly—"

"The worst part was finding his skin under my nails. I scrubbed them until I ran out of soap, but I can still feel the slime." She spoke too fast, like someone on the verge of losing control. "It was the first time I had touched him in more than three years, Nathan. How about that? This is a real night for firsts. Give me the helmet. We don't want to be late."

"The hell with that, I'm taking you to a doctor."

"No!" She grasped his arm. "I'm fine. We need to go to the airport. We have to get that shipment."

Her hand was trembling, but her grip had the strength of desperation. Nathan looked at her wrist. The cuff of her blouse had fallen back. A bruise marred the skin there, too. Were there bruises on her arms where he'd caught her? He felt sick at the realization he'd caused her pain. "He won't hurt you again," he said through his teeth. "I swear it."

Her gaze searched his and her grip tightened. "I believe that, Nathan. I do. I don't care how you make your living, you're different from him."

Her trust humbled him. She still didn't know the truth. "Kelly—"

"You said you wanted to help me."

"I will."

"Then help me now. Whatever your real agenda is makes no difference to me, as long as we move that heroin. You were right about everything. I don't want to be here. I've never wanted to be part of Stephan's business, but he gave me no choice."

He covered her hand carefully. He felt no satisfaction at having his assumptions about her innocence confirmed. He should have ignored her protests and done something yesterday, before she got hurt. "Hang in there, Kelly. It's going to work out. All you have to do is wait—"

"No! I can't wait. We have to leave for the airport now. I have to make sure those drugs get delivered to Stephan just as you promised. It's the only way—" Her voice broke on a sob. A tear fell on his hand. "It's the only way to get my son back."

Thunder rumbled in the distance. Despite the muggy air, he felt a chill. "Back?"

"Jamie's gone. Stephan took him away." She lifted her face. Pain, stark-naked and soul-deep, shone from her gaze. "I never even had the chance to kiss him goodbye."

Chapter 8

Kelly wasn't sure when it had started raining. She hadn't noticed she was getting wet until Nathan pulled the bike to the shoulder of the road, took his slicker from one of the saddlebags and helped her put it on. For the past twenty-four hours, she hadn't eaten and she hadn't slept. She had been swinging between surges of utter panic and periods of detached numbness. The thought of what Jamie must be going through froze her heart, yet it was the only thing that gave her the strength to function.

The bike sliced through the puddles on the pavement, sending spray arching from the tires. Water squelched from Nathan's soaked shirt as she locked her hands around his waist. She shivered, sheltering behind his back as he took the exit for the airport. The rain was coming down so heavily, the lights were reduced to blurs. He took the winding route he'd used before, but instead of concealing his bike behind the main Pack Leader warehouse, he steered directly to the square building in the center of the complex.

Nathan parked a few feet in front of the side entrance, tucked his helmet under his arm and punched a series of numbers into the keypad over the door lock.

She slid off the seat and removed her helmet. "What are we doing here?"

Lightning flashed across his face, sparkling from his wet skin and sharpening his harsh features. The rumble of thunder that followed sounded like the Harley. "Come with me," he said, yanking the door open. He had parked so close, the door barely cleared the bike.

"You told me you're a driver. Shouldn't you go where they keep the trucks?"

"I need to check something here first." He caught her hand to pull her over the threshold with him, then cursed and immediately loosened his hold. "Damn, did I hurt you?"

"What? No." She laced her fingers with his and followed him inside. "Don't worry about me. Those bruises are nothing. All that matters is Jamie."

The corridor was empty, as it had been the other time she had been here with him, but Nathan made no attempt to walk quietly. His boots thudded on the tile as he turned toward the elevator instead of the stairs. When they reached the top floor, he led her down another hall, this one covered with a thick gray carpet. In places, the walls were glass, revealing darkened offices on the other side. Nathan passed them by and stopped in front of a wood-paneled door at the end of the hall.

There was a keypad beside this door, too, but it was

no obstacle to Nathan. His fingers flew over the numbers with what looked like practiced ease. The lock clicked. He swung the door inward and reached around the door frame.

Light flooded the room from recessed pots in the ceiling. It was obviously an office, but it was private and more luxurious than any they had passed. The far corner consisted of windows, giving a blurred panorama of the airport lights through rain-streaked glass. The other walls were rich, paneled wood. A large, mahogany desk was positioned in the center of one wall, along with a row of blank monitors. Across from it were armchairs, a couch of deep burgundy leather and a glass-topped table that held a foot-high wood carving of a baying wolf.

Kelly hesitated on the threshold, looking at the brass plaque that was fastened to the door. N. R. Beliveau. President. "Uh, Nathan…"

"It's all right, Kelly," he said. He tugged her into the room and swung the door closed. "We're safe here. No one's going to bother us."

"What are we doing here?"

"Regrouping," he said, taking her helmet from her hand. He hung it along with his on a wooden coat-tree behind the door, then helped her out of the slicker he'd loaned her and hung it beside their helmets. "Go sit down, I'll get you a towel."

She'd been able to tuck the slicker around her legs almost to her calves, so only the ends of her hair and her feet were wet. Unlike Nathan. He was soaked from head to toe, dripping a puddle where he stood. "Stop worrying about me," she said. "You need a towel more than I do. What time is it?" She looked around for a clock. "The flight's due to land at midnight. We have to make sure we get that load."

"The flight's probably delayed by the weather. I'll check the status."

Nathan walked to the monitors that were lined up behind the desk and pushed some switches. The screens came to life almost instantly, filling with lines of data. He unbuttoned his wet shirt and peeled it off as he studied the numbers. "It's what I thought," he said, tossing his shirt on the large swivel chair that was behind the desk. He slicked the excess water from his jeans with his palms and squatted to open a cupboard door that was set beneath the monitors. "The whole schedule is backed up. Nothing's getting through. This is going to buy us some time to work things out."

"What's there to work out?" She stared at his naked back, then glanced nervously at the door behind her. She knew he had nerves of steel, but this was too much. "I don't like this, Nathan."

He took a gym bag out of the cupboard, unzipped it and withdrew a thick white towel and a black fleece jogging suit. "We'll be fine, Kelly."

"How can you say that? I don't want to risk—"

"It's okay," he said. He left the clothes on the desk and came over to drape the towel around her shoulders. "There's no risk. This is my office."

His bare chest filled her vision. His skin was damp, gleaming over a magnificent expanse of taut muscles. It took her a second to register what he'd said. "Why are you lying? I saw the sign on the door. This office belongs to someone called Beliveau, the president of the company."

He lifted one corner of the towel to blot the moisture from her face, carefully avoiding the bruise on her jaw. "It's my door and my sign. And those are my sweats that

I'm about to change into." He returned to the desk and unzipped his jeans.

Kelly drew in her breath and turned her back. There were a pair of thuds as he yanked off his boots, the sucking noise of sodden fabric and then silence. With disbelief, she realized that he must be completely nude.

It didn't alarm her. She had more important things to worry about.

But, good Lord, he was only a few feet away.

"I'm sorry, Kelly," he said, his voice muffled. "You've got enough to deal with right now, but this is something you deserve to know." He paused. There was the slide of soft cotton against skin for a few moments. "Damn, there's no easy way to tell you this."

"Tell me what?"

"I am Beliveau."

She spun to face him. Except for his bare feet, he was once more fully clothed, in a black jogging suit that fit his long legs and broad shoulders perfectly. She clutched the ends of the towel he had given her. "I don't know what kind of game you're playing, but this isn't the time."

"I agree, this is no time for games, so I'm not going to continue this charade. Now that I know the truth about you, there's no longer any reason why I can't tell you the truth about myself."

She felt a chill. "Truth?"

"My name is Nathan Beliveau. This is my office. I founded Pack Leader Express."

"That's impossible."

"I realize it's a shock, but—"

"I know you're Nathan Rand. I checked out your reputation myself."

"I was Rand. I became Beliveau when I quit stealing cars."

Her head was reeling. The lack of sleep was clouding her brain. She fisted her hands in the towel. "Are you saying this entire courier company is a front for your smuggling business?"

"I'm making a mess of this," he muttered. He came over to put his hand on the small of her back and guided her to the couch. "Sit down and I'll try to explain."

She sat for the simple reason that her knees gave out. The panic was threatening to return. Had she been wrong to confide in Nathan? He sounded completely rational, but what he was saying didn't make sense.

The cushions dipped as Nathan sat beside her, stirring up the scent of leather from the couch. It reminded her of his jacket, and it was oddly steadying.

"Everything I've told you about my past is true," he said. "Everything, Kelly. My childhood, my crimes, all of it. I never lied about that. Nathan Rand was the name I was born with. Beliveau was the name my great-grandfather adopted when he left the Sioux to live with his wife's people. I took his name when I moved to Chicago ten years ago because I wanted a fresh start."

All right. That much did make sense. He'd changed his identity because he'd wanted a fresh start. She could understand that. It was the same thing she and Jamie would have to do if they got away... No. *When* they got away.

"Have you heard of a man named Tony Monaco?" Nathan asked.

"Monaco? The name's familiar. I might have heard Stephan mention him. Why? What does he have to do with any of this?"

"Tony's family used to run a criminal organization

that was more powerful than Volski could imagine in his wildest fantasies. Now Tony runs a group called Payback. He finds people on the wrong side of the law and helps them move to the right side. I was one of the first members."

She played that back in her head. Could she have heard him correctly? "The right side of the law? Do you mean you went straight?"

"Completely. Pack Leader Express is totally legitimate. Everything I have now, I've earned honestly."

The pride that rang from his voice was unmistakable. She glanced around the office, recalling the way he'd entered the combinations for the door locks, his familiarity with the room and the computer equipment. Her gaze fell on the carving of the wolf. It was exquisitely detailed, evoking the haunting mystique of the lone predator. It was just like the Pack Leader logo that was printed on the left side of Nathan's sweatshirt.

It was the wolf that did it. More than once, Nathan had reminded her of one. Could it only be coincidence that the founder of Pack Leader had chosen that particular animal as his talisman? It all fit so well, what other explanation was there?

Maybe it was a consequence of stress, but this wasn't that big a leap for her mind to take. Her heart had told her all along that Nathan wasn't as bad as he'd seemed.

Could her heart have been right?

For the first time in twenty-four hours, she felt a glimmer of hope. "You're not a criminal," she said.

"Not anymore."

"All this is really yours."

"Yes, it is. For now," he added.

She took another look around the office. Her initial

relief at his revelation faded. "Are you in financial trouble? Is that why you want to smuggle Stephan's heroin?"

"Not exactly."

"Well?"

"It's complicated."

She flung out her arm. "And this isn't?"

He caught her hand and cradled it between his. "We don't have time for the long story, so I'll give you the short version. I posed as Rand to pay my debt to Tony. It's what I agreed when I joined Payback. In exchange for the help Tony gave me, I promised to even the score by bringing another criminal to justice."

"Even the score?"

"It's the whole point of Payback." He shifted closer, his gaze steady on hers. "Kelly, I never intended to smuggle anything. That heroin was intended to be the bait in a sting that would deliver Volski's entire organization to the FBI."

There had been so many shocks, this one took longer to sink in.

But it fit, too. She'd sensed at their very first meeting that Nathan wasn't interested in the money the heroin would bring him. She'd even felt that Nathan was honorable. That's why she'd let him kiss her in the warehouse....

The warehouse where she'd gone through the charade of explaining how they would transfer the perc. While she'd been tormented by her conscience over her plan to double-cross him, he'd been planning to double-cross *her*.

He'd lied and lied well. What else had he lied about? She yanked her hand from his and sprang to her feet. "Does this mean you're a cop?"

"Hell, no."

"What's the difference? You were going to set us up for them."

"I was prepared to do whatever it took to pay my debt."

"I could have been arrested along with Stephan."

He rose from the couch. "That was a possibility, but I didn't want it to happen."

"Sure, that's easy to say now, but—"

"Kelly, why do you think I kept pushing you about your relationship with Volski? How many times did I ask you whether or not you were a willing participant?"

"How was I supposed to know why you were asking? I thought you were just stirring up trouble or looking for a way to use me to get a better deal."

"I felt all along you were innocent, but you kept acting guilty."

"I had no choice. I believed you were Stephan's partner."

"And I believed you were his girlfriend."

"Until tonight, that bastard hadn't touched me for more than three years. We don't even live in the same wing of the house."

"You put on a good show."

"It stroked his ego to let people believe that, and it allowed me to stay with my son. Why didn't you tell me the truth, Nathan?"

"Why didn't you?"

What was she doing? She had no right to criticize him. None whatsoever. Logically, she knew that.

But he had kissed her, knowing he could be responsible for sending her to prison.

Then again, she had kissed him, fully aware that she planned to use him as a scapegoat.

But she wasn't going to use him as a scapegoat any longer. She'd decided that yesterday and now she'd had to abandon her plan completely. She had canceled the duplicate pickup she'd arranged. The barrels with the heroin weren't going to be incinerated, they were going to be unloaded from the cargo plane and taken to the freight warehouse where they would be waiting exactly as Nathan thought they would be. She wasn't going to double-cross anyone.

Only, Nathan had never intended to deliver that heroin, either. It was the bait in a trap with the FBI.

She slapped the heels of her hands to her temples. Her head was spinning again. "No," she murmured. "Oh, God. This can't be happening."

He stroked the hair from her forehead, his touch butterfly-light on her skin. "I didn't suspect the truth until I saw you with Jamie. I've already arranged immunity for you, Kelly. All you have to do is cooperate and Volski won't hurt you again."

"He has Jamie."

"We'll get him back for you. The FBI will track him down and—"

"No!" She dropped her hands and stared at Nathan. Finally, the full import of his revelations struck her. "My God, Nathan. You can't mean to go through with it now. You have to deliver those drugs exactly as you agreed. You have to call off this sting. Tell the FBI you made a mistake."

"It's too late to call it off, Kelly. The FBI know what's happening. Volski's warehouse will already be surrounded. The feds have people around the airport, too. They'll be watching me from the minute I leave here with the heroin."

Backing up, she bumped into one of the armchairs and reached behind her to steady herself. "No, you don't understand. We have to do what Stephan says. It's the only way I'll get Jamie back."

"Once Volski's men get arrested, someone will tell us where Jamie is."

"They won't! They're all terrified of Stephan."

"The police—"

"Don't talk to me about the police!" She changed direction and advanced on Nathan. She jabbed her index finger into his chest. "Don't you think I would have gone to them years ago if I believed for one minute that they could help me? They can't."

"Kelly…"

"It's been twenty-four hours. Jamie probably isn't in the country anymore."

Nathan muttered a short, pungent oath.

"Stephan's been holding this over my head for three years. It's why I never went to the cops." She jabbed him again. "He has properties all over Russia. Jamie could be at any of them. Even if we find out where he is, I couldn't legally get him back. Stephan still has family there, and he's vindictive enough to launch an international custody case, even from prison." She leaned closer, flattening her palms against his sweatshirt. "By the time I saw my son again he would be all grown up. Is that what you want?"

"Of course not."

"Then call off this sting. You have to deliver Stephan's heroin."

"Kelly." Nathan's tone was firm, but there was a gentleness in his voice, a sympathy that warned her she wouldn't like what she was about to hear. "Even if I could call it off, even if we managed to sneak the drugs past the FBI and arrange some other way for Stephan to get the shipment, once he has the drugs in his possession, do you really think he would keep his word and reunite you with Jamie?"

It was the last piece of the truth, the final blow she hadn't been prepared to take.

Of course, Stephan didn't intend to keep his word. He never had kept his word to her, right from the start. He knew her weakness and used her love as a tool. It wouldn't matter to him whether or not he was killing her one day at a time. He didn't care about what was best for Jamie—he only cared about himself.

Stephan had her exactly where he wanted her. After she did this for him, there would always be the next deal, and the next one after that. She would never escape. She would be another Alex Almari, doing Stephan's bidding, too broken in spirit to rebel…only no bandage would stop this bleeding.

A future without Jamie unrolled in front of her with soul-wrenching clarity. She was caught between Stephan and the FBI. Putting her faith in either of them wouldn't bring her son any closer.

Her only option left was the man in front of her.

Kelly lifted her hands to Nathan's face. She skimmed her fingertips over the hard lines of his jaw, his high cheekbones and his broad forehead, tracing the evidence of his warrior heritage, absorbing the feel of his strength. "I've never begged in my life, Nathan, but if you want me to, I'll go down on my knees. I'll do anything you ask. Anything. Just help me get my baby back."

Lightning streaked the sky, flashing a split second of brilliance through the wall of rain. The control tower in the distance was etched with white, the row of planes that sat at the gates gleamed silver and the pavement writhed with puddles. Thunder rattled the glass in the windows, vibrating through Nathan's palm along his arm and straight down to the soles of his feet.

He hadn't needed to check the weather bulletins that scrolled across the center monitor to know the storm was a bad one. For the past hour and a half, nothing had moved. But something was moving now. He could see the pinpricks of headlights from baggage trams near one of the passenger terminals. The airport was stirring, coming back to life. The intervals between the lightning and thunder were growing longer. The storm was receding. The landings would resume in a matter of minutes.

He looked at the freight warehouse to his right. Activity wouldn't have stopped there, in spite of the storm. The sorting and loading would have continued fullsteam as the night crew would use the respite from incoming material to get ahead, preparing for the onslaught of work once the storm ended.

This was his place, the life he'd established. It was more than a business, it was his proof that he'd reinvented himself. Until ninety minutes ago, he'd believed that he would do anything to keep it. It still wasn't too late to change his mind.

He adjusted his focus, moving his gaze to the reflection in the glass. Kelly was pressed into the corner of the burgundy couch, her knees drawn up and her feet tucked beneath her. Her hair had gone curlier as it had dried. It cascaded over the arm cushion in a mass of reddish gold as her head lolled sideways, giving her an air of innocence, even though the neckline of her silk blouse had gaped, exposing part of her right breast. She had dozed off thirty minutes ago. She was going to be stiff when she woke up, but sleep was a mercy. She needed as much as she could get.

There was an old saying about being careful what you wished for. From the first moment he'd heard Kelly sing, Nathan had been hoping to see her as she really was. He'd wanted her to drop the act and show him the feelings he'd known she kept inside.

Tonight she had done just that.

He pushed away from the window and turned to face her. Yes, he'd wanted to see her true emotions, but not like this. He hadn't wanted to see this proud, strong woman reduced to the point where she would beg.

He'd never known anyone like her. Everything she did, she did out of pure love for her child.

Compared to that, worrying about losing a few bucks didn't seem important anymore.

Okay, it was more than a few bucks. Tony didn't run a charity. He'd already given one warning and his patience was running out. If Nathan didn't go through with this sting, he risked losing everything.

Yet if he went through with it as planned, Kelly would likely never see her son again.

She'd been right. The chances of winning an international custody case when the boy was already out of the country were slim. Even within the country, the legal system didn't always work. Jamie would be left to the mercy of people who were aligned with Volski. Who knew what kind of hell the child would have to endure? He was only three. He'd have no chance of protecting himself.

The image of a smiling boy with strawberry-blond hair sprang to his mind. Gradually, the image turned into the picture of a scrawny, black-haired runaway who had learned to survive on the streets of Detroit. That's what could happen to a child without a defender. Nathan's circumstances had been different from Jamie's, yet the end result could be the same. Kelly was right to worry about that, too.

Nathan's hands twinged. He realized he was clenching his fists again. He flexed his fingers to get his circulation flowing and glanced at his watch.

It *was* too late to change his mind. It had been too late the first time he'd seen Kelly hold her son. No, it had been earlier than that. He should have known this would happen back in the warehouse when he'd held Kelly in his arms and had felt her tears on his skin. Hell, he'd known she'd be trouble the second he'd seen her walk up to the microphone in the Starlight.

He punched Templar's number into his phone and lifted it to his ear. "There's been a delay," he said when he heard her answer.

"The weather?"

"Yes. It will be another four hours at least before I can load up."

"I've sent two extra units to the airport to cover you. Until the storm clears, it's too dangerous to use the choppers."

"Make sure your units hang back. If Volski's people see someone tailing me, he'll rabbit."

"We know our jobs, Mr. Beliveau. All we need is for you to do yours."

"Is Volski still in his warehouse?"

There was a pause. "Yes."

"How many men are with him?"

"We've counted twenty-seven in the building and he

has lookouts positioned around the neighborhood. Don't worry, we're on him."

"Stand by. I'll call when I'm on my way."

He terminated the connection and walked to the monitors. Arrival times were beginning to appear on the screen that displayed the cargo schedule. He scanned the flight numbers. Yes, there it was. Flight 2112 from Beijing by way of Vladivostok. It must have been at the front of the queue. He'd probably be able to see its lights within minutes.

He dialed another number.

Naturally, Stephan wouldn't answer his own phone. The voice that came on belonged to Dimitri Petrovich.

"It's Rand," Nathan said. "Tell Volski the flight's about to come in."

"We know this already," Petrovich said. "We have been checking with the airport."

That was what Nathan had figured, which was why he hadn't lied about this to them. Volski probably had people stationed around the airport just like the FBI did, and for the same reason. They would be monitoring Nathan's progress as soon as he left. "It will be another four hours at least before I can get the shipment loaded on the truck."

There was a brief conversation in Russian, then Volski's voice came through the receiver. "Mr. Rand," he said. "Take good care of my property."

Nathan gritted his teeth. Merely hearing the bastard's voice made him want to punch something. "Absolutely," he said. "Those drums won't get a scratch."

"Scratch," Volski muttered. He spat out something in Russian that was probably a curse. "As for my other property, do see that she is returned in working condition when you finish."

Nathan cut the connection and somehow restrained himself from crushing the phone in his fist.

There was no time to indulge his temper. He had to move fast. He called the dispatch desk in the communication center next and told them what he wanted, then went to his wall safe and took out the envelope that held his emergency cash. He regarded the switchblade that had lain beneath it. He'd locked that knife away a lifetime ago, yet he picked it up without hesitation and slipped it into the side pocket of his jogging pants. When his preparations were done, he walked to the couch and gave Kelly's shoulder a gentle squeeze.

She lifted her head and stretched sleepily, widening the gap in her neckline. For a second, her face was slack with confusion. She looked around the office until her gaze steadied on him. The confusion fled and stark pain filled her eyes. "Jamie," she whispered.

He braced one knee on the cushion beside her and cupped her right cheek in his palm. "He'll be okay, Kelly."

She pressed her lips together, her nostrils flaring as she fought for control. She nodded once and leaned into his caress.

The gesture moved him more than he would have believed possible. Without pausing to think, he eased her face toward his and kissed her.

Nathan didn't bother trying to tell himself the kiss was to comfort her. Even Beliveau wasn't that noble. He'd needed to do this for days.

Her mouth trembled under his, then finally softened. He could taste the dried salt from her tears on his tongue.

I'll do anything you ask. Anything.

The memory of her plea hummed through his blood, kicking his pulse, turning his breathing ragged. He wouldn't be male if he hadn't thought about it. The physical pull had been there even before he'd known the truth about her, but now it was tangled with other urges, feelings that were unfamiliar yet just as primitive.

They had known each other a week and he had seen her child for only a few minutes. Why did he feel as if they were his to protect, to fight for, to hold?

Hell, it had to be the situation. It would mess with anyone's head.

He broke off the kiss before he did more and leaned his forehead against hers. Only the worst kind of bastard would take advantage of her now. "Kelly, I can't call off the sting with the FBI."

She drew back her head, her protest already forming. "Nathan—"

"Wait, let me finish. Cooperating with the FBI is the only way you'll get immunity and the best way I can keep my promise to Tony." He paused. "So I can't call off the sting, but I can delay it."

Hope flared across her face. "Why? What are you going to do?"

"First I'm going to steal Volski's dope." He took her hands and pulled her to her feet. "Then I'll trade it for your son."

Chapter 9

Kelly twisted on the seat as she watched the blurry outline of a road sign slide past. Even at the rate this truck was traveling, it would be another ten minutes before they were clear of the city. The thunder was receding, but the rain was unrelenting. In a few hours it would be dawn.

Was it raining where Jamie was? He didn't have his rabbit. Had he managed to fall asleep anyway? Had Gloria remembered to leave a light on for him? Was there anyone with him who cared about his comfort?

"Are you cold?" Nathan asked. He took his hand from the steering wheel and reached forward to switch on the heater. "The dampness should disappear in a few minutes."

Her teeth chattered. Kelly knew it was from nerves, not cold. She latched on to Nathan's voice to pull herself back from the loop of her thoughts. It was far too easy to wallow in her worry, but that wouldn't do Jamie any good. She couldn't afford to fall apart, especially now. "I'm okay."

"If you put your shoes under the blower vent, they'll dry faster."

It was a practical suggestion, and she was grateful for it. Although several hours had passed since that motorcycle ride in the rain, her shoes were still soggy. She toed them off and pushed them into the stream of warm air that flowed from beneath the dashboard, then drew her heels onto the seat and wrapped her arms around her legs.

The dark gray Pack Leader Express windbreaker Nathan had provided for her enveloped her like a blanket. A matching baseball cap concealed most of her hair. At a distance, with her outline blurred by the rain that streaked the windows, Kelly would appear to be just another uniformed driver like Nathan.

Or like the other four teams of drivers who had pulled out of the Pack Leader warehouse with them.

She looked at the red taillights of the truck they had followed onto the expressway, then glanced at the side mirror. Headlights sparkled from the truck behind them.

The best way to smuggle anything is in plain sight.

That was what Nathan had told her a week ago, before she'd learned he wasn't really a smuggler. But that's what they were now, in spades. They were moving a load of heroin under the noses of both Stephan and the FBI. The sheer daring of what they were doing was incredible. "Are you sure this convoy of decoys will work?" she asked.

"It will improve our odds." He checked the readout on the dashboard clock. "When the other trucks start to peel away, Volski won't know which one to follow. Neither will Templar. With so much of their manpower concentrated around Volski's warehouse, neither of them has the resources to tail all of us. I would have liked to use more decoys, but these were the only trucks available."

She peered into the mirror again. The truck behind them had fallen back, its turn signals flashing. It changed lanes and headed for an exit. Kelly craned her neck to watch the road. She had no way of knowing whether or not it was only coincidence, but two sets of headlights followed the truck to the off-ramp.

"The storm works in our favor," Nathan continued. "The FBI choppers are grounded. The spray from the pavement makes for poor visibility on the road. There's a chance we'll slip through without any trouble."

"And if we don't?"

"My drivers think they're taking part in an efficiency test, so they'll cooperate fully if they're stopped. The only thing they're guilty of is wasting fuel by driving around in an empty truck."

"What if we're stopped, Nathan?"

He adjusted the wiper speed and rubbed the film of condensation from the side window with his sleeve.

"Nathan? What if the FBI or Stephan's men try to stop us?"

"They won't be able to. Nothing smaller than a tank is going to stop a fully loaded tractor trailer going sixty miles an hour."

That hadn't been a boast, Kelly realized. His tone had been as matter-of-fact as when he'd been discussing the weather.

Why shouldn't he be confident about his driving abilities? He had probably become skilled at evading pursuers when he'd made his living stealing cars. God, she hoped his skills wouldn't be put to the test. "They might not be tracking us, anyway. We did leave two hours earlier than you told them we would."

"I thought moving out early might make them scramble, but it probably didn't fool anyone."

"Sure, it would. You told me that with so many shipments, another one wouldn't make a ripple. Moving this load out ahead of schedule—"

"Wouldn't have worked without a smoke screen like these decoy trucks are giving us," he said. "A guy as paranoid as Volski would be watching for a double-cross. That's why he ordered you to keep track of me."

Taillights blinked in front of them. The truck ahead changed lanes for the next exit. Kelly tightened her hold on her legs as she watched it go. "Are you saying that if there hadn't been any storm and everything had run on time, and someone had scheduled a second, earlier pickup for this load it wouldn't have worked?"

"Absolutely not. Even without accounting for Volski's paranoia, I would have noticed something was wrong as soon as I checked the schedule on the monitors in my office. I oversimplified our procedures when I told you about them last week. We have checking mechanisms built into the system. There's no way anyone could have gotten this load ahead of me." He looked at her. "Why are you asking?"

Tell him!

She bit her lip, trying to stop the voice in her head. It would be smarter to keep quiet and leave well enough alone, but her conscience wasn't easy to silence. Nathan was using the resources of his company to help her. He wasn't Rand, he was Beliveau, the president of Pack Leader Express.

There had been so many revelations, that part hadn't fully sunk in.

Still, she didn't doubt he was who he said he was. The evidence was overwhelming. In addition to what she'd seen in his office, the people they had encountered in the communication center and the men in the warehouse who had loaded the truck had recognized him and addressed him by name. While they had regarded her with curiosity, their manner toward Nathan had been respectful and cooperative.

Yet even knowing who he was, to Kelly, Nathan still looked and sounded like the man she'd known as Rand. He might be a successful—and legitimate—businessman, but there was an edginess to him, an aura of leashed energy that set him apart. Try as she might, she couldn't picture him sitting behind a desk.

One thing was clear, though: her situation with Jamie was pushing all of Nathan's buttons. That had to be the reason he was so willing to go to such lengths to help them. He believed she was an innocent victim, coerced into working in Stephan's drug business, but if Nathan knew how she'd set up this deal because she planned to betray him, there was a possibility that he might have second thoughts about what he was doing for her. What good could come of telling him now?

"Kelly?" Nathan stretched out his arm to touch his fingertips to her cheek. "You're crying again."

She blinked impatiently. Although her nap in his office had revived her, she still hadn't been able to bring her emotions under control. "Until I met you, I never cried," she said. "Not in front of people, anyway. I couldn't let anyone see what I felt or what I thought."

"It's how you survived."

She drank in his quiet understanding. "Except when I was with Jamie, or sometimes when I sang, my life was one long lie. The only hope that kept me sane was the thought of getting away, but whenever I tried to leave, Stephan's people tracked us down."

He rubbed the corner of her eye with his thumb before he put his hand back on the wheel. "It must have been hell."

"Each time they brought us back, things got worse. I couldn't go home to Maple Ridge because Stephan threatened to hurt my family if I did. I couldn't go to the police because I wouldn't know who was on his payroll and he has video of me setting up a dope deal that he threatened to use against me. On top of that, he has proof of Jamie's paternity and he could have taken Jamie out of the country and—" She hiccuped. "And he already has. How could I have been such a fool?"

"There's no point blaming yourself, Kelly."

She pressed her face to her knees. "I can't help it. I'm not proud of the things I've done."

"Whatever you did, you did for your son."

Oh, God! This man couldn't truly be as kind as he seemed, could he? Men simply weren't like that. She dried her eyes on her pant legs and turned her head to study him.

The glow of the dashboard lights left deep shadows on his face. Lit from below, his features looked harsh, uncompromising and incredibly masculine, reminding her of the way he'd looked the night they'd met. And just as at that moment when he'd first touched her hand, she felt a thrill chase across her nerves.

Despite where they were and what was happening, Kelly wanted to kiss him. More than that, she wanted to crawl onto his lap and wrap herself around him. Fit her body to his and feel his heartbeat against her skin.

Adrenaline. Stress. Lack of sleep. There were plenty of rational explanations for her urges. She had to remember that. It was natural that she would feel strongly about this man because he was helping her get Jamie.

Yet she couldn't prevent the jolt that went through her when he glanced over to find her watching him.

As if he could feel her thoughts, his gaze moved to her lips. Her mouth tingled with an echo of that tender, sensuous kiss they had shared in his office...and her body throbbed with the memory of those charged, sexy kisses he'd given her as Rand.

Kelly curled her nails into her palms. What was wrong with her? She shouldn't be thinking about *any* man while her son was missing. What kind of mother was she?

Nathan jerked his gaze back to the road. "Is your seat belt fastened?"

His sudden question made her frown. "Yes. Why?"

"We may have a problem."

Light flared through the truck cab. A vehicle was coming up fast in the passing lane, its headlights glaring from the mirrors. Seconds later, the large boxy shape of a black Navigator swerved in front of them. The headlights of the truck picked out the silhouette of a lone occupant, a heavyset male.

Nathan blasted the horn.

The Navigator's brake lights flashed as it slowed down. Nathan checked his mirrors and changed lanes to pass it, but it matched his speed and swerved in front again.

He reached for the gearshift. "You'd better brace yourself, Kelly. It looks like someone realized we're not heading for Volski's warehouse."

She let go of her legs, put her feet on the floor and shoved them back into her damp shoes. "Nathan, what—"

"Hang on!"

The engine stuttered as he geared down to reduce the speed of the truck. He wrenched the wheel to the right. Car horns sounded behind him as he steered across the traffic to the exit they were passing. "We've got to get off the expressway," he said. "We'll have a better chance of losing him on the streets."

Kelly anchored her hands on the shoulder strap of her seat belt as the truck took the ramp. To their left she could see the Navigator overshoot the exit. It skidded into a 180-degree turn and accelerated into the oncoming traffic. One car fishtailed and rolled over as its driver tried to get out of the way. Two more cars collided and spun across the lanes but the bulky SUV plowed through the wrecks to reach the exit. She lost sight of it as Nathan guided the truck down the ramp, yet she didn't doubt it was somewhere behind them.

"That has to be one of Volski's men," Nathan said, continuing to work the gears as he drove beneath an overpass. "The feds wouldn't risk civilian casualties like that."

A gas station and a strip mall flew past. The expressway had been heading south through the suburbs, but Kelly couldn't tell exactly where they'd come out. The street was wide and mercifully deserted. She winced as Nathan sped through a red light.

"Can you tell how many are back there?" he asked.

She pressed close to the window and squinted through the glare in the side mirror. Headlights bored beneath the overpass and appeared on the street behind them. At first, it looked as if there were at least two sets, but then she realized she was seeing reflections on the wet pavement. "Only one."

"We'll have to make this quick before he calls for reinforcements. They wouldn't be able to stop me, but I don't want them to follow me."

They went through a second red light. As soon as they had cleared the intersection, Nathan hit the brakes. The trailer jackknifed, sending the entire rig skidding sideways down the center of the street. Kelly screamed and curled her arms over her head.

Their momentum carried them past a grocery store parking lot and a Home Depot before Nathan gunned the engine, threw the tractor back into gear and swung them to face the way they had come.

Kelly blew out her breath and risked a glance out the windshield. The Navigator had slowed as it had followed them and now idled halfway down the block. The driver had probably been anticipating a crash. He wouldn't have expected a challenge.

Nathan worked his way up through the gears, revving the engine until it roared. Within seconds, they were hurtling directly at the stopped SUV.

The driver had no chance to turn around. He swung into the parking lot of the grocery store. Nathan followed, bounced over the curb and rammed the Navigator from behind, sending it crashing into a row of grocery carts that were lined up in front of the store.

Nathan hauled on the wheel. The cab missed the debris by inches but the trailer sideswiped the rear of the

Navigator as they passed. The force was enough to knock the SUV over the carts and through the store's plate-glass window.

Air brakes screeched as Nathan executed a tight turn and brought the truck to a shuddering halt. The instant they stopped moving, he jumped to the pavement and sprinted back to the store through the rain.

Kelly gasped for air, her pulse racing. She'd seen car chases in movies, but the choreographed mayhem on the screen was nothing like the short, brutal pursuit that had just occurred. Nathan's skill as a driver was phenomenal—she hadn't known it was possible to handle a truck the way he had. By the time she managed to get her seat belt unfastened and had climbed down, Nathan had reached the wrecked SUV.

An alarm was clanging somewhere inside the store. Shards of glass, pieces of insulation from the wall and twisted shopping carts lay everywhere. The front and the back ends of the bulky Navigator were crumpled beyond recognition, but the sides were almost intact. Nathan braced one heel on the frame and yanked open the driver's door.

Kelly recognized the driver. It was one of Stephan's men, a bouncer at the Starlight who had tried to give Nathan a rough time the week before. He appeared to be shaken up rather than injured by his collision with the grocery store. He took one look at Nathan, then fumbled to shove the deflating air bag aside and reached into his jacket.

Even as Kelly shouted a warning, Nathan caught his arm, pulled him out of the vehicle and spun him face-first into its side. A gun dropped onto the pile of debris. Nathan kicked it away and twisted the man's arm up his back. "I want you to take a message to your boss for me," he said.

"What the hell are you doing, Rand?"

"Tell Volski I want an even trade. His heroin for Kelly Jennings's son. You got that?"

"You're friggin' crazy."

"Tell him I'll call him with the details."

"He'll kill you for this."

Nathan turned the man to face him and gave him a look. It was as inscrutable as it was deadly. The color slowly drained from the man's cheeks.

Nathan released his hold. "Volski isn't going to kill anyone," he said. "If he wants his dope, he'll do exactly what I say."

Almost two months had passed since Nathan had driven down this track. It had been night then, so while he'd known the brush along the sides was thick enough to block out the lights from the highway, he hadn't seen the extent of it in daylight. Branches that his bike had passed beneath the last time he'd been here slapped wetly across the windshield of the truck or snapped off against the mirrors. No vehicle this size could have come this way in years. He cut his speed to a crawl— the puddles that filled the ruts concealed potholes deep enough to rattle his teeth.

He glanced at Kelly. She'd taken off her hat when they'd turned off the highway, yet the hair that tumbled around her face couldn't fully hide the purple discoloration on her jaw. Her knuckles whitened as she gripped the seat belt to steady herself against the rocking of the cab. Her determination to see this through was in every line of her body.

"This is going to work," he said. "It's the last place that anyone would think to look for us."

She jumped as a branch smashed into the side window. "I know. Your reasoning makes sense."

She was a courageous woman, Nathan thought. Choosing Latchford as their destination was a bold move. Until a month ago, Volski had been in partnership with a local crime boss named Sproule, bringing in heroin from Asia by hiding it in shipments of outboard motor parts.

That deal had ended with Sproule's death when every law-enforcement agency in the country had descended on the area to help dismantle the Sproule organization. Volski hadn't come near this small, southern Illinois town since.

From what Nathan had heard, Latchford was still crawling with feds, so Templar wouldn't expect him to drive into the eye of the storm. Volski wouldn't, either.

Yes, the reasoning was sound, but to pull this off, Nathan was going to need help.

He worked the wipers to clear off the leaves that stuck to the windshield and finally spotted the rusted chain-link fence with the broken gate that marked the entrance to the abandoned gravel pit. The brush opened up to reveal an expanse of gray sky.

Nathan let the engine idle as he took stock of his surroundings. The ground sloped away in front of them to a bowl-shaped depression ringed by crumbling, weed-choked banks. This track was the only way in, and the floor of the pit was far enough below the rim to conceal anything down there. Unless an FBI chopper flew directly overhead, no one was going to spot this rig.

Nathan moved his gaze to the tire tracks he'd been

following since he'd left the highway. They led down the ramp in front of him and across the center of the pit to a parked black pickup.

A tall man leaned against the fender of the pickup, the sides of his long black raincoat flapping loosely against his calves. His ankles were crossed casually and his hands were hooked into the front pockets of his faded jeans. Even from a distance, Nathan recognized the familiar stance.

"Is that your friend?" Kelly asked.

"That's him." Nathan eased the semi forward and nosed it down the ramp. "His name is Cooper Webb. He's a former member of Payback."

Cooper watched them approach until they had rolled to a stop a scant yard from the front bumper of his pickup, then pushed himself upright and walked over to Nathan's door. Coal-black curls brushed the upturned collar of his raincoat and black beard stubble bristled from his jaw, giving him the appearance of an outlaw. As usual, his ice-blue gaze gave nothing away.

Nathan climbed down from the cab and held out his hand. "Thanks for coming, Webb."

"I knew you'd show up sooner or later, Beliveau." He shook Nathan's hand. His movements were fluid and his grip firm—the bullet wound in his shoulder had apparently healed well. "Last time I saw you, you said I owed you a favor."

"That's right, you do."

Cooper gestured to the trailer. "Your rig's looking banged up. You want me to give you some driving tips?"

Nathan glanced behind him. There was a minor dent in the side of the trailer where he'd given the SUV with Volski's man a second tap. It wouldn't have affected the cargo—he'd made sure his warehouse crew had strapped the barrels down so securely they couldn't have moved. "That wasn't the favor I had in mind."

"What do you need, Nathan?"

"For starters, I need another truck, smaller than this one, bigger than yours."

"*You're* asking *me* for a truck?"

"That's right."

Cooper shrugged. "Okay. You buying or leasing?"

"I can't guarantee I'll return it, so I'd better say buying."

"I'll make a few calls and see what I can do."

"Good." He reached inside his windbreaker for his envelope of cash, withdrew some of the larger bills and handed them to Cooper. "I'll also need security for this trailer and everything in it. This cash should cover that, too."

"No problem. The guys are doing a job for me right now, but nothing that can't wait. They're always happy to get extra cash." He focused on the money and raised one eyebrow. "A hundred grand?"

"If you need more, let me know."

"What have you got in that rig?"

"A stolen shipment of dry-cleaning chemicals and two tons of Stephan Volski's heroin."

Cooper whistled softly between his teeth as he folded the bills and tucked them into a front pocket of his jeans. "So you smoked Volski out, after all."

"Not yet, but I will."

"That load should do it."

"The way the dope's packed in barrels, we'll need welding equipment to extract it."

"I know where we can, ah, borrow some." Without

taking his gaze from Nathan, Cooper tipped his head toward the truck cab. "What about the redhead you got riding shotgun? You need security for her, too?"

"No, thanks. I'll be looking out for her myself, but we will need a place to stay out of sight while I set things into motion. I'd appreciate it if you could drop us off at a motel."

"Are you expecting trouble?"

"Not as long as no one knows where we are."

Cooper considered that for a while. "We're rebuilding my bar on the site of the old one. It won't be finished for another week, but the air's on and the plumbing's hooked up. If you don't mind roughing it on the floor, you can't get a better location than that for privacy."

Nathan nodded, pleased by the suggestion. The Long Shot had been on the northern edge of the Latchford city limits, set back from the highway and far from any neighbors. If Cooper had built the new place anything like the last one, it would be as secure as a fortress. "Sounds good."

"We'll take that wad you're carrying downtown and scare up a mattress."

"Better make it two."

"Two?" Cooper's eyes crinkled with the hint of a smile. "You sure you don't want some driving tips, Nathan? Maybe that hog you like to ride is bad for your plumbing."

"I'll manage."

"Suit yourself. Who is she, anyway?"

"The mother of Volski's child."

Cooper sobered fast. "Does Tony know about this?"

"Not yet."

"Oh, man. What the hell did you get yourself into?"

Nathan wasn't sure of the answer to that one. It was why he'd avoided asking the question himself.

Chapter 10

The smell of fresh wood and primer paint hit Kelly the moment she entered the building. Sheets of plastic draped the stacks of chairs and small round tables that lined one wall of the main room. Wooden crates stamped Fragile stood under the windows. A sawhorse, power tools and pieces of lumber lay in the center where the bar would be. According to what Nathan had told her, when it was completed the Sure Thing was going to be almost identical to Cooper Webb's first bar, the Long Shot, but that completion was going to be delayed. The men who had been working on it were currently busy on the other side of town, guarding Stephan's heroin.

"Watch out for the cord, Kelly."

Kelly shifted the shopping bags she carried to one side so she could see the bright orange extension cord

Hayley Webb had pointed out. "Thanks, Hayley." She stepped over the cord and followed her past a plastic-draped pool table. "I appreciate you letting us stay here."

"No problem," Hayley said over her shoulder, echoing what her husband had told them that morning. "We wanted to wait until the loft was painted before we moved in. It has a long way to go yet, but it's in better shape than the downstairs. Kelly, are you sure you can manage all those bags? Maybe you should leave some for a second trip."

She shook her head. The bags were filled with clothes and other necessities she had bought during a quick stop at the Latchford Mall. "I'm fine. They're not too heavy."

Hayley led the way to a hall through an empty door frame—the door that would eventually fill it was leaning against a pile of two-by-fours. "Oh, this is such a mess. I'm sorry we don't have any extra room in our current place or you and Nathan could have stayed with us."

"It's probably safer for you if we don't."

Hayley reached the foot of a staircase of unfinished wood and turned to face her. Tall and graceful, with angelic blond curls and hazel eyes that seemed on the verge of a smile, she was a startling contrast to her raven-haired, tough-guy husband. "I know all too well what men like Stephan Volski are capable of, Kelly, but someone has to take a stand against them when the law doesn't work. What you're doing is very admirable. I only wish I could help more."

To her chagrin, Kelly felt tears fill her eyes yet again. She'd only met Hayley this morning, yet she was fast becoming a friend. Hayley was an open, compassionate woman, her feelings easy to read on her face. She had been quick to grasp the danger Kelly and Nathan were in, and she hadn't hesitated to offer her help along with her sympathy.

After being alone for so long, all this sudden support was hard to take. Kelly fought to keep her composure. "Thank you."

Hayley smiled, shifted the bags of food she carried and started forward once more. "I'll show you upstairs while we wait for the boys."

The boys. Kelly knew she had meant Nathan and Cooper, but it was strange to hear them referred to like that. It seemed too familiar, too...normal, as if this were an ordinary get-together and she and Nathan were a couple.

She parted her lips to explain their relationship, but she really didn't know what to say. Figuring out where she stood with Nathan, or what she felt about him, hadn't been a priority. She followed Hayley in silence.

After the chaos on the main floor, the loft that stretched across the back of the building appeared an island of calm. Apart from the kitchen appliances that were built into an alcove in one corner of the large room, there wasn't a stick of furniture. The hardwood floor was bare and the drywall was unpainted, yet the place didn't look bleak, thanks to the view from the row of windows that made up one wall. The clouds that had lingered from the storm of the night before had finally broken up, and the tops of the trees outside were brushed with gold from the setting sun.

Was Jamie having supper now? Or was he having breakfast? What time zone was he in?

Kelly forced herself to focus, setting down her bags near the door. Hayley moved past the breakfast bar that

angled out from the wall to the kitchen area and stored
the food in the refrigerator. Nathan and Cooper arrived
a few minutes later with some of the new bar stools from
downstairs, then returned to the pickup and brought
back the packages of bedding Nathan had purchased.
For their final two trips, they carried a pair of mattresses
into the apartment and put them beside the wall opposite the windows.

Kelly tried hard not to stare at the mattresses. They
were queen-size and luxuriously thick, but she would
have been fine with a blanket on the floor. Comfort was
the least of her concerns, yet Nathan hadn't blinked at
buying the best, even though they wouldn't be used for
more than a few nights. He also hadn't blinked at buying two instead of one.

With everything else going on, she shouldn't feel
awkward about the issue of their sleeping arrangements.
Why shouldn't he buy two beds? She kept forgetting
that Nathan Beliveau was a wealthy man.

He leaned over to slit the plastic that covered one of the
mattresses. He was still wearing the black jogging suit he'd
put on in his office the night before. The back of the sweatshirt pulled up, baring a strip of skin at the base of his spine.

Kelly did her best not to stare at that, too. That's why
it took her a minute to realize the wealthy Nathan Beliveau was using a switchblade to cut through the plastic.

"No one's going to bother you here," Cooper said.
His deep voice echoed from the bare walls. "Make sure
you keep away from the windows if you turn on a light."

Nathan nodded. "It's been a while since I was on the
run, but I know the routine."

"Yeah. Just try not to burn the place down while
you're here."

Nathan tugged off the plastic and folded it into a square. "Not a chance," he said, his lips twitching. "I couldn't do that as well as you."

"There are a lot of things you can't do as well as me. You sure you don't want me to give you some tips?"

Nathan flipped his switchblade into a spinning arc in front of him, caught it by the handle and moved to the second mattress. "I told you, I'll manage."

"Sure. It's a big floor."

Hayley moved to join Cooper by the door. "What are you two talking about?"

Cooper slipped his arm around his wife's shoulders. He looked at the floor, then looked at her and gave her a lopsided smile. "Seeing this place got me thinking about the time we spent in the last one."

A flush rose on her cheeks. "Behave yourself, Cooper."

"But you like me bad."

Her eyes sparkled as a silent communication passed between husband and wife.

Kelly was taken off guard by a wave of longing. The love that flowed between this unlikely couple was obvious, and they made no attempt to hide it. Seeing it warmed her like the sight of the sunshine touching the treetops beyond the windows. Even after Cooper and Hayley had said goodbye and the door had closed behind them, their love seemed to linger in the air.

Kelly had once dreamed of having love like that herself. She'd wanted it so much, she'd ended up with Stephan Volski. It had been her own naive dreams that had set her on this path, her own bad judgment that had led to losing her son.

Had he eaten at all today? Had Gloria remembered that he liked to keep his food in separate piles on his plate?

Kelly grabbed one of the stools that the men had brought from downstairs and moved it to the breakfast bar. She needed to keep busy. "Did you call Stephan yet?" she asked.

Nathan finished stripping the plastic from the second mattress and put away his knife, then straightened up and rubbed his jaw. He hadn't had the chance to shave. Seeing the day's beard stubble on his cheeks seemed strangely intimate to Kelly. It was the kind of thing a lover would see.

"No," he replied. "I haven't called him yet."

"Why not?"

"I need to give Templar the chance to regroup before I arrange the meet with Volski. She wasn't pleased to be left hanging in the wind."

"You didn't tell her where we are, did you?"

He paused. "No, Kelly. I told you I wouldn't. And just in case she tries to locate us by tracing the call, I don't intend to phone her again until we're on the move."

"She's still going to cooperate, isn't she?"

"Templar wants Volski. That outweighs her annoyance with me. She understands I'm still her best bet for setting him up."

She put the stool down and went to pick up another. "But if arresting Stephan is her priority, how can we be sure the FBI won't move in until I have Jamie?"

"For the sting to work, the FBI need to catch Volski and his people actually in possession of the heroin, and I won't be giving it up until your son is safely in your arms."

"But—"

"It's a matter of timing, Kelly, and I'm good at schedules. I do run a courier company."

"Can we trust this FBI agent? Nathan, what if she's the one who's on Stephan's payroll? Or what if she lets this slip to someone who is?"

"Derek Stone vouched for her."

Derek was the man Nathan had met at the Painted Pony. Yet another member of Payback. Yet another lie that she hadn't suspected. She carried the second stool toward the kitchen. "Can we trust him?"

"Tony Monaco does. That's good enough for me." He regarded her for a while, his amber gaze warm with sympathy, then turned and walked to one of the bags he had left beside the door.

"What are you doing?" she asked.

"You must be exhausted," he said, carrying the bag to the mattresses. He pulled out a blanket, tucked it under his arm and continued to go through the bag until he came up with a pillow. "Not counting the nap you had in the truck and that one in my office, how long has it been since you slept?"

She glanced at the window and shook her head. "It's still early. I couldn't possibly sleep now."

"Then try to eat something." He dropped the bedding on one of the mattresses, then went past her to open the refrigerator. "Hayley brought some food."

"You go ahead. I'm not hungry."

"You sure? There's a barbecued chicken and a container of salad."

"I couldn't eat," she said. "Did Cooper's people get the heroin out of the barrels?"

He closed the fridge. "Not yet."

"We have to get it out." She braced her hands on the edge of the breakfast bar. "We can't move it in the barrels again. That would be too obvious."

"They didn't finish draining the perc until this afternoon." He faced her across the width of the counter. "They only had enough time to cut into half the barrels. It would be better to wait until tomorrow to do the rest."

"Why?"

"The gravel pit's off the highway, but I don't want to run the risk of someone noticing the lights."

"We should be there."

"Cooper's men are guarding it."

She smacked her palms on the counter. "We should guard it, too. We're not doing any good here."

He reached out to cover her hands with his. "We wouldn't do any good there, either."

She snatched her hands away. "There has to be something we can do."

"There is. We can take advantage of this time to rest."

"No. I can't."

"Kelly, you're too wound up." He rounded the breakfast bar and caught her shoulders. "You have to try to relax."

"Relax? How am I supposed to do that?"

"We're safe here. No one except Cooper and Hayley know where we are. I realize the place is rough, and it's not going to be as comfortable as what you're used to, but—"

"How can I care about my comfort when I don't know where my baby is or what he's doing or whether he's crying or hurt or hungry or—" She snapped her jaw shut, pushing her tongue to the back of her front teeth. The panic was never far away. All it took was one unguarded moment and it was ready to engulf her.

Nathan massaged her shoulders. "He'll be all right, Kelly."

She pressed her lips together and nodded once.

"He knows you love him. That's going to give him strength."

She backed out of his grasp and crossed her arms. "Don't," she said.

"What?"

"I can't take kindness right now, okay?"

"Why?"

"Because I'm trying very hard not to fall apart."

"You won't." He brushed her hair behind her ear. "You're an exceptional woman."

"Please, stop."

"It's the truth. You're so tired, you're swaying on your feet, but your only thoughts are for your son."

He was wrong. Her only thoughts *should* be for her son, but she was also thinking of how she could feel Nathan's body heat. She inhaled slowly, drawing in the familiar male musk that rose from his skin. "He's all I have," she said. "He's my life."

"He's lucky to have you for a mother."

"That's where you're wrong, Nathan. If I hadn't been such an idiot by falling for Stephan, none of this would have happened."

"We all make mistakes, Kelly. Stop beating yourself up about it."

"But it's because of me—"

"It's because of you that your son is the happy, confident child I met in the garden," he said firmly.

His words were as soothing as his scent. They were exactly what she needed to hear. Her chin trembled. "For God's sake, that's enough."

"What?"

"If you keep being nice, I'm going to cry again and

I don't want to wallow in this. It's selfish and it won't help Jamie."

He moved closer. As naturally as breathing, he put his arms around her and pulled her into his embrace. "If anyone's being selfish here, it's me."

"You? Nathan—"

"I've been waiting all day to hold you. I don't give a damn what you say, I'm not waiting any longer."

She laid her hands on his chest to steady herself. She could feel the contours of his muscles through the fleece. Instead of pushing away, she absorbed his strength.

"Kelly, I realize you're going through hell, but whenever I see that sheen of tears in your eyes, all I can think of is having you in my arms like this."

She rubbed her forehead against his shoulder. "You feel sorry for me."

"I feel a lot of things, but pity isn't one of them." He stroked her hair. "You have a deep well of passion inside you. It's there in everything you do and it's drawn me to you from the start. That's what I see in your tears. I see your passion. You make me wish I was a better man."

"A *better* man?" She tipped back her head so she could see his face. "You're doing so much for me already. I still can't believe the risk you're taking to help Jamie and me. You've made yourself a fugitive."

"Only temporarily. That will get straightened out when I complete the sting with Templar." He tucked a lock of hair behind her ear. "Besides, we all need help sometimes."

"I wish I had trusted you sooner."

"That works both ways. I should have gone with my gut and trusted you."

"But you have, Nathan. You've been so kind."

"Is it kind to want to kiss you when you're hurting?"

"Kiss me?"

He touched his index finger to her lower lip.

The contact made her shudder.

"I know I shouldn't." He pressed lightly, coaxing her lips to part. "This is the last thing you need."

Her pulse began to throb. Her emotions were already raw and her control was paper-thin. It wouldn't take much for her to lose it completely. She moved her head. "Nathan…"

"You see, if I was a better man, I wouldn't be thinking about kissing you."

"A kiss…" She swallowed. "A kiss can be comforting."

"That's the problem. I don't want to comfort you. I want to put my tongue into your mouth and taste you."

The stab of need took her unawares. Her fingers clenched, crumpling his sweatshirt. She focused on his lips.

"You're a beautiful woman, Kelly. All you have to do is walk into a room and my palms start to sweat. It's more than the way you look, it's what you are inside." He trailed his fingertip over her chin to her throat. "Do you remember the night we met?"

She remembered every second of the time they had spent together. Vividly. Often. She nodded, and his hand moved lower.

"That dress you wore drove me crazy. I was trying to set up the most important deal of my life and there you were with all that slinky gold plastered to your body. When you leaned over the table and gave me that glimpse…" He tightened the arm he held around her back. "You have no idea how hard it was to keep my hands off you."

"But you touched my breast anyway."

"I'm only human." He slid his thumb beneath the edge of her blouse to stroke the curve of her collarbone. "Did you like it when I touched you there, Kelly?"

Her nipples tightened painfully. Her pulse was hammering now. The way he was holding her, she was having trouble getting air into her lungs. Not because his grip was too tight, but because each breath she drew brought her breasts more fully against his chest.

When had worry switched to desire? And did it matter? Something other than grief was making her heart race, and it made her feel...alive. She arched toward him. "Yes," she murmured. "I liked it very much."

"I knew you were putting on an act. So was I. But your skin was like warm satin and I wanted to feel more."

"It was all part of the game. I couldn't understand why it felt good."

"It felt so good I thought I was losing my mind." He lowered his thumb to the valley between her breasts. His voice roughened. "Even when there were lies between us, this much was honest."

"Yes."

"I'm not a good man, Kelly."

"Nathan—"

"Because the decent thing to do right now would be to let you go but I don't know if I can." His eyes darkened. "Do you *want* me to kiss you?"

Adrenaline. Stress. Lack of sleep. She reminded herself of all the rational explanations that she'd thought of before. "I shouldn't."

"That's not what I asked." He smiled. "Do you want me to kiss you?"

She rarely saw him smile. It wasn't hard to believe,

considering all they had gone through together, because there hadn't been much to smile about. Yet when he did, oh, it was like daylight breaking through a storm. His lips curved, deepening the grooves that framed his mouth. The dimple appeared in his cheek and the corners of his eyes crinkled. He was without a doubt the most devastatingly handsome man she had ever seen.

Oh, yes. She wanted his mouth on hers and she wanted his touch on her body. She didn't want to think anymore, she wanted the oblivion he was offering. She framed his face in her hands, lifted herself on her toes and gave him the only reply she could.

She opened her mouth over his, sealing their lips while she used her tongue to taste him the way he'd said he wanted to taste her. Sensations slammed through her, positive emotions, not negative, as she asserted the power of being female. She tilted her head, finding the right angle, as if they had done this for a lifetime.

The moment stretched, a breathless instant as he let her do what she wanted. Kelly could sense his restraint in the tension that hummed through his frame and in the firmness of his lips. Somehow, he understood how much she needed to feel the choice was hers.

She moaned, thrusting her fingers into his hair to pull him closer, but Nathan needed no more urging. While the sound she'd made still echoed in her throat, he bent her over his arm, slipped his fingers beneath the edge of her bra and closed his hand around her breast.

The frank possessiveness of his caress made her gasp. Delight streaked through her body as his thumb found her nipple. While his tongue probed her mouth, he circled and stroked, his caress keeping time with his kiss.

She clung to his neck as her knees buckled. Before

she could fall, he swept her into his arms and started across the room.

Nathan knew he couldn't pause to think. If he did, his conscience might stop him and he couldn't let that happen. The feel of Kelly so warm and willing in his arms was stirring urges that were far deeper and more primitive than thought.

Kelly didn't lie passive in his embrace. She kissed his neck, his jaw, anywhere she could reach. She was so eager for his touch, she started undressing before they reached the mattress. Her blouse was half off, baring her shoulder and the top of her arm. He halted beside the nearest mattress, came down on one knee and tried to finish the job, a task made more difficult because Kelly was so intent on taking off his clothes. She tugged his sweatshirt over his head and threw it behind him, then closed her teeth on his shoulder and pushed his jogging pants past his hips.

Fabric ripped as they got rid of the rest. Nathan had a twinge of regret as he spread out the blanket. The king-size bed in his penthouse was custom-made to fit his height and his bedroom. It had Egyptian cotton sheets and a satin-covered down-filled duvet. Kelly deserved more than a mattress on the floor.

Yet she seemed unaware of the surroundings. With her hair tumbled over her shoulders and her gaze steady on his, she knelt naked in the center of the blanket and cupped her hands under her breasts.

The invitation shredded what remained of Nathan's restraint. He came down on top of her, straddling her legs as he eased her to her back. He took what she offered him, using his lips at first, slow and easy, exploring every dip and curve. He opened his mouth, tasting and teasing with his tongue as her skin warmed and her nipples hardened, then he settled himself more comfortably and started using his hands.

"Nathan…" Her hips moved beneath him as she curled one leg around his waist. A tremor went through her body. "Nathan, that's…ah…"

He relished the honesty of her response, just as he reveled in the sound of his name on her lips. Her pleasure was heightening his own, driving him closer to the edge. He pressed his palms to the sides of her breasts and traced his tongue along the valley between them.

Kelly grabbed his head, her nails digging into his scalp, her breath coming in sharp gasps. "Oh!"

He moved his hands together, rolled her nipples between his fingers and thumbs and gave them a sharp squeeze.

She arched off the mattress, a surprised cry in her throat as she convulsed beneath him. "Nathan!"

Even though every nerve in his body pulsed with demands to finish this, Nathan felt a glow of satisfaction as he watched her climax. Damn, she was more woman than he could have imagined.

She looked at him, her eyes glazed and her pupils huge. She wrapped her fingers around his biceps. "Oh," she breathed. "What…?"

He parted her legs with his knees and slid between her thighs. "Let's see what else you like."

She smiled, then gave him a shove to roll him to his side. "No, let's find out what you like."

Nathan groaned as he felt her mouth on his chest. The slide of her hair across his skin was sweet torture. There was no hope of regaining any restraint, but he strove to hold out as long as he could.

Her exploration of him was sensual yet guileless, a mixture of passion and innocence. She was stimulating him on levels that went beyond sex, yet when she slid her fingers around his erection and her hair brushed his thighs, the need to complete what they had started became painful. He left her only long enough to dump the rest of the bag of bedding on the floor and rip open the box of condoms that had been in the bottom of it.

No, he wasn't a good man. He'd hoped all along that this would happen. That's why he had bought the condoms. But if he was a bastard for taking advantage of her, then he was going to be one hell of a happy bastard.

They came together with enough force to jerk the mattress into the wall. The room echoed with the sound of their rapid breathing and the slap of skin on skin. Pleasure built on pleasure until Nathan felt Kelly's final climax ripple around him, triggering his own release.

At last.

Something simple.

It must have been a nightmare. Yes, of course. Her baby wasn't really gone. She could hear him crying. There, on the other side of the wall. Kelly whipped aside the blanket and rolled out of bed.

But the floor was too close. Her ankle crumpled beneath her and she fell to her knees, her palms striking bare wood. She shook the hair out of her eyes and lifted her head. Colorless, predawn light seeped through a bank of windows, revealing a room she didn't recognize.

Her heart pounding, she scrambled to her feet and ran forward. Her sole slipped on a piece of plastic and she stumbled sideways, knocking into a wooden stool. It clattered to the floor with a noise that made her jump. "Jamie?" she called. "Baby, where are you?"

There was a rustle of movement behind her. "Kelly?"

That was Nathan's voice. What was he doing here? She had to warn him to get away before Stephan caught him.

Bare feet padded across the floor. "Kelly, wake up," he said.

She turned toward him. She had a split second of confusion when she saw that he was naked, but then he had reached her and was pulling her into his arms. Her lungs filled with his scent, her body softened at the familiar feel of his and reality came back with a rush.

This wasn't her bedroom. It was the loft over the Webbs' new bar. She was in Latchford, not Chicago. Jamie really was gone.

And Nathan was naked because they had spent most of the night making love.

She waited for the guilt, but it didn't come. Yes, she loved her son, his welfare was more important to her than her own, yet she couldn't regret what she and Nathan had done. It had felt too natural, too necessary for regrets.

Simply because she was a mother didn't mean she had stopped being a woman.

"You had a bad dream," he said. His voice rumbled through his chest, tingling across her skin.

She dropped her forehead to his shoulder. "I thought I heard Jamie crying."

"He'll be all right, Kelly." He stroked her back. "You have to believe that."

"I do. If I didn't, I'd go crazy."

He kissed the top of her head and swayed gently where he stood, lending her his strength as easily as he'd given her his passion.

She turned her head, her gaze going to the windows. The sky looked fathomless, the stars that remained were impossibly far away. Was it still night where Jamie was? Or was it already this afternoon?

She slid her arms around Nathan's waist and nuzzled her lips against his chest. The panic that had propelled her from her dream faded. She kissed the spot above his heart, taking the feel of his heartbeat into her mouth, and the emptiness in her own heart eased. When she felt him stir and harden against her belly, she took his hand and followed him back to the mattress.

They made love gently, quietly, his thrusts evoking only murmurs instead of screams, yet it was enough to keep the world at bay, at least until the dawn.

Chapter 11

Nathan paced across the loft, the phone pressed to his ear. It was fortunate there was so little furniture—if there had been more, he would have kicked it. "Why the delay, Stephan? Don't you remember where you put him?"

"The boy is my blood and you insult me, Mr. Rand." Volski's tone could have cut glass. "I have had men killed for less."

"You're wasting time," Nathan said. "We do the exchange tonight."

Kelly slid off the bar stool where she'd been sitting and pressed her fingertips to her mouth, her gaze riveted on Nathan as he went by. She had pulled her hair into a ponytail this morning, so he could see the bruise from Volski's blow was continuing to fade—it was only a pale blue shadow now. Her other bruises, the ones on her arms and her wrists, were healing more quickly. They were tinted with yellow and barely noticeable.

"That would not be convenient," Volski said.

"You'd better make it convenient if you want any of my heroin."

"Those goods are mine, Rand."

"By the way, how are your customers taking this delay, Stephan?" He pivoted when he reached the windows so he could keep Kelly in sight. She took a few steps forward, her bare feet whispering against the hardwood floor. Nathan tried not to let the sight of her hips molded by the new blue jeans she'd bought the day before distract him. "They've waited almost two months for you to bring in this shipment," he said. "How much longer do you think they'll wait before they look for another supplier?"

There was a simmering silence.

"Maybe you've forgotten that I know who your customers are," Nathan continued. "I can cut you out. A hundred percent profit sounds better than the thirty-five you offered me last week."

Another silence. When Volski spoke again, his accent had thickened. "Tomorrow. Midnight."

"Fine. I'll let you know the place."

"You are a fool, Rand. It never had to go this far. We could have made a deal for the bitch if I had known you were that interested."

Nathan braced his fist against the window frame. He was thankful Kelly couldn't hear the other end of the conversation. "Keep it up, Stephan, and I start selling your dope."

"She isn't worth this. She has you hot for her now but you'll find she doesn't get better with use. You made a bad bargain."

"Then you won't have any trouble meeting my price."

"She is nothing but a tease, Rand. That body of hers makes promises she doesn't keep." Volski laughed. "Or perhaps I was correct when I suspected your tastes lie in a different direction from women."

Nathan terminated the connection before he could hurl the phone across the room. He wasn't by nature a violent man, but hearing that bastard insult Kelly was more than he could take, no matter how ludicrous Volski's claims were.

Kelly lowered her hands from her mouth. Her fingers were shaking. "He agreed to the trade?"

"Yes."

She closed her eyes and drew in a deep breath. "Thank God," she whispered.

He wasn't proud of the way his gaze dropped to where her breasts swelled against her lilac-colored T-shirt. He usually had better self-control than that. The night before was over, he couldn't afford to dwell on it. He needed to keep a clear head now more than ever. "Hang on. I've got one more call to make." He dialed another number, then lifted the phone back to his ear.

It seemed to ring forever before Derek Stone's familiar drawl came on the line. "You've reached On the Edge Tours. Leave a message. If I get back alive, I'll get back to you."

Nathan frowned. "Derek, this is Nathan Beliveau. If you're there, pick up."

The line clicked. "Hey, chief."

"What have you got?"

"Whoa, no 'Hello, how you doing' first?"

"Volski's going to do the trade tomorrow night. Have you made any progress?"

"Not much." Derek's tone turned all business. "I've

been keeping my ear to the ground since you called Friday night. Volski's people are all stirred up, but I haven't found a pattern. I can't tell you for sure whether the kid is still in the country."

"Damn."

"I'll stay on it, but I can't promise anything. It's been seven years since I did this kind of work."

"Weren't you any good?"

"Don't try some psychological challenge bull on me. I've got nothing to prove. I know I was the best."

Nathan pinched the bridge of his nose. "I appreciate your help."

"You'd better. The first favor was on Tony. This one's not free, Nathan."

"I understand. I'll owe you one, Derek."

He grunted. "Just so you know, Templar's people are all stirred up, too. You have some balls taking that dope from under her nose. She's looking for you."

"She'll know where I am when I phone her tomorrow."

"You'll have to watch your step until then. She can get mean when she's crossed."

"Mutual interest can outweigh mutual trust," Nathan said, recalling what Kelly had told him the week before. "Templar should know that she'll get what she wants soon enough."

"Uh-huh. Let's hope we all do."

Nathan finished the call and put away his phone. If this didn't work, he was going to have some powerful enemies, but he'd chosen his path and wasn't about to back out now. He walked over to Kelly and took her hands in his. "Are you okay?"

Her eyes misted. "It sounded as if Derek wasn't able to find out where Jamie is."

"I wish I had better news." He rubbed his thumbs across her knuckles. "Derek's going to keep trying, but I don't want to give you false hope. Following through on this exchange with Volski is still our best bet."

"I know. I'm grateful your plan's working, but…"

"But what?"

"Nathan, what kind of man would trade his son for a load of heroin? Stephan's a monster for using him this way."

"You'll get no argument from me on that."

She blinked hard, as if impatient with her impending tears. She'd been that way since she'd awakened this morning. No, since the second time she'd awakened. The first time, she had allowed her storm of emotions to rage free.

"What did he say that made you so angry?" she asked.

"It was nothing. Just his usual boasting."

She pulled away and walked back to the bar stool. Instead of resuming her seat, she braced her hands on the edge of the breakfast bar and dipped her head. "It worries me. I did everything I could to shield Jamie from the world we were living in. I tried to give him as normal a life as possible, but what if Jamie inherited that… evil? What if he turns out like Stephan?"

"Kelly—"

"God, I wish he wasn't Jamie's father."

He thought about that for a while. "There was never any doubt, was there?"

She shook her head. "You saw Jamie's eyes."

"What color were Marty's eyes?"

"Marty?" She looked at him over her shoulder. *"Marty?"*

"The boy next door in Maple Ridge. He was your boyfriend before Volski, wasn't he?"

She turned, pressing her back to the bar. She stared at him.

He saw the caution descend on her gaze and he felt like kicking himself. Could he have broached the subject any more clumsily? "Let me explain. Volski claims he can prove his paternity, but that doesn't mean he told the truth. If it's possible that Jamie could have been fathered by someone else, that would be an advantage if the issue of custody ever did come up."

"My God," she muttered. "This would be funny if it wasn't so pathetic. Nathan, there's no doubt Jamie is Stephan's."

"Okay."

"I never slept with Marty."

"You…"

"There's never been anyone else."

His gut contracted as if he'd been punched.

"I told you I waited for Marty, didn't I?" she asked. "I meant that in every way. I lived with my parents, I worked in my dad's grocery store and I spent my spare time at choir practice or planning my wedding. I would have worn white." She gave a mirthless laugh. "I was a virgin when I left Maple Ridge. A twenty-two-year-old virgin. Can't get much more pathetic than that."

He walked toward her. "I'm sorry. I didn't mean to hurt your feelings, I was only trying to be practical."

"When I met Stephan, it was like a fairy tale. He was handsome and elegant and was going to help me make my dreams come true. And they were pathetic dreams. Love, a family, a chance for a singing career. I can't believe I was that naive."

"Kelly—"

"I thought Stephan was my Prince Charming.

He thought I was a whore. I guess that's what you thought, too."

"Stop it." He reached out for her. "You know I've never believed that about you."

She swatted his hand away. "Do I?"

"Yes, you do. Only right now you're pissed off with me for the insensitive way I brought up the subject of your previous sexual experience." He cupped her shoulders. She tried to shrug off his touch, but he hung on. "For that I apologize."

She pressed her lips together and looked past him.

"Kelly, you're the most passionate woman I've ever met." He moved his head, trying to catch her gaze. "That's why I just assumed…"

He paused. He didn't want to think about any other man touching this woman, especially a man like Volski. That bastard wouldn't have been gentle with the gift Kelly had given him. He wouldn't have treated her with the respect she deserved.

Nathan tightened his grip. No, he couldn't think about that. When he did, it stirred something primal and ugly inside him that he'd prefer to leave alone.

Yet who would have guessed that a woman as extraordinarily sexy as Kelly could be so inexperienced? And since Volski had been her only lover, and they hadn't been together for more than three years, that meant *no* man had touched her since before Jamie's birth. Who could imagine she would have remained celibate for so long?

Still, the clues had been there. The aura of innocence that mixed with her sensuality. The singing that was an outlet for her passion. The way she channeled all her energy into her love for her son. Volski's disinterest in her.

The surprised look on her face yesterday when she had climaxed the first time.

Had it been the first time?

A surge of possessiveness caught him off guard. Nathan moved his hands to her face. "Kelly, look at me."

She looked at his chin.

"Please," he added.

Her gaze lifted to his.

Damn, he must be a pig, he decided. He had spent the night satisfying his needs with her, he'd just upset her, and all he could think about was making love to her again. Seeing her respond to his kiss. Feeling her tremble. Making her *his*. "It doesn't matter to me what you did in the past. I told you before, I would never judge you."

"Yes, that's what you said."

"I lost my virginity when I was twelve years old because I had wanted to prove to my gang that I was a man. It was quick and meaningless and it's not something I'm proud of, but that's the world I was living in. I learned a long time ago regrets are useless. They don't change a thing."

"I realize that."

"Yet you've done nothing to be ashamed of. You were alone and vulnerable and you trusted the wrong man, that's all." He stroked her cheek with the backs of his fingers. "You might have been living in Volski's world for three years, but his taint didn't stick."

"You don't know me well enough to say that."

"Sure, I do. I've heard the honesty in your voice when you sang. I've felt it each time we kissed."

"Honesty?" Her breath hitched and she ducked away from his touch. "You have no idea, do you?"

"What?"

"I lied to you from the minute we met."

"We've been through this before. I understand why you thought you had to play the role you did."

She shook her head and moved to the center of the room. Her ponytail bounced with her steps, making her look achingly young. Her hips swayed, making his hands itch. Nathan hooked his thumbs in his waistband and tried to concentrate on what she was saying.

"No, you don't understand," she said. "I wasn't going to tell you, but there doesn't seem to be much point keeping quiet about it now. After all, you slept with me. That has to count for something."

The brittle tone in her voice was back. Nathan's first impulse was to go to her and take her in his arms anyway, but he had a feeling she needed to talk. "What we shared last night was special, Kelly. We both wanted it."

"Let me finish this, okay? You're only making it harder." She squared her shoulders and faced him. "Nathan, I realize you have this whole protectiveness thing going with me. You think that I was a victim, but I wasn't waiting to be rescued when you came along."

"What do you mean?"

"It's why I turned down your first offer to help. I didn't need to risk trusting you because I had my own plan to escape Stephan."

"How? You told me he kept Jamie a virtual prisoner."

"That's right, he did, but I had figured out a way to beat his security. I was going to take my child and run. It would have been my last chance, because I knew if Stephan caught me, he would have ended my access to Jamie. He might have ended my life. I didn't care. I knew I couldn't go on any longer. You were the key to the whole thing."

"How?"

"The heroin deal I set up with you was going to serve as a distraction. I planned to destroy the drugs before you could pick them up and make it look as if you had double-crossed Stephan. While he went after you, I would disappear."

For the second time in as many minutes, events clicked in Nathan's mind. There had been clues to this, too. Odd moments with Kelly, cryptic comments, inexplicable flashes of guilt. They hadn't made sense before.

Now they did.

Of course, Kelly wouldn't have been waiting to be rescued. She had too much spirit to remain anyone's victim. And she was desperate enough to use any means at her disposal, to make an impossible choice....

Once again, Nathan felt as if he'd been punched. But this time, the blow went deeper than his belly. The warmth he'd been feeling faded. "Volski would have tried to kill me. He might even have succeeded, because I wouldn't have seen it coming."

Her hands fluttered. They often did when she was agitated. "I'm sorry, Nathan. I didn't want that to happen but I was aware it was a possibility."

He struggled to process the information logically, but his gut continued to churn. She had fooled him completely. She had lied and lied well. What else had she lied about?

But he had lied to her, too. He had no right to be angry. Damn, he couldn't think straight.

"It probably won't make much difference to tell you I had changed my mind," she continued. "I had decided to warn you after I got Jamie away, to give you a fighting chance. It doesn't really matter that my scheme wouldn't have worked anyway, either. I'm not trying to excuse—"

"You were going to betray me."

His shout echoed in the empty room. He hadn't meant to raise his voice. There had been a lot of things he hadn't meant to do lately, but he didn't seem to have any control when it came to his feelings for Kelly.

She lifted her chin and regarded him defiantly. "Do I need to point out that you were planning to do the same?"

"Not the same, Kelly."

"No? You had your own agenda, too. You were willing to see me arrested."

"You can't compare me setting you up for the FBI with you tossing me to Volski."

"If I had gone to prison, what would have happened to Jamie?"

"I didn't know about Jamie at first. When I found out, I offered to help."

"How could I take your offer? I couldn't trust you. I didn't even know your real name."

"You trusted me enough to kiss me."

"That wasn't trust, it was hormones."

He raked his hands through his hair, trying to rein in his temper. Neither of them was in a position to throw stones, yet somehow he found himself launching one more volley. "Was it hormones that made you plead for my help when you came to me on Friday?"

"I was out of options, Nathan. And for my son, I would do anything."

Yes, he'd known that. He'd admired that. He found her devotion to her child one of her most attractive aspects. He should put aside his wounded ego over her deception and try to regard this logically.

But then his gaze went past her to the mattress they had shared.

I would do anything.

Was that what last night had been about?

You slept with me. That has to count for something.

He'd known she was vulnerable, but what if she'd thought he'd *expected* her to sleep with him? Did she think that was the price for his help? Was that why she'd said he must have thought she was a whore?

Nathan wanted to kick something, but there was nothing within range. He wanted to yell again. Instead, he strode to Kelly. She stepped back, but he followed and grasped her by the hips to pull her against him. Her scent filled his lungs, her breasts molded to his chest and his anger switched instantly to desire.

No, he couldn't have been wrong about this part. It was still simple. The intimacy they had shared last night had to have been genuine. Even Kelly wasn't a good enough liar to fake that, was she?

She moistened her lips. "Nathan, what are you doing?"

He braced his legs apart and splayed his fingers, cupping her buttocks and angling her hips to fit their bodies together. Then without any preliminaries, he brought his mouth down on hers.

He held nothing back. His pulse was already pounding, his muscles tensed. His senses were heightened and his patience gone. He wouldn't give the doubts a chance to grow.

He never had any doubts when he kissed her.

Kelly caught his shoulders. He could feel her nails bite through his shirt. Instead of retreating, she met his wildness with her own. The kiss turned fierce and carnal as she gave as much as she took. They only stopped when they ran out of breath.

Her head fell back. "I thought…" She gasped for air. "I thought you were mad."

He grazed her earlobe with his teeth. "I am. I'm furious."

She wriggled, rubbing her stomach across the bulge behind his fly. "Is that what you call this?"

He lifted her off her feet and backed her across the floor until her shoulders hit the wall. Using his chest to hold her in place, he reached between them to open his fly and lower the zipper on her jeans.

"Nathan, I'm mad at you, too."

He stroked the edge of her panties. "Yeah, I can tell."

She laughed. It was low and throaty and the most erotic sound he'd ever heard her make. She rubbed the back of his calf with her foot, her eyes half closing.

He kissed her again. She shifted her hips to help him push down her jeans, then kicked her clothes aside and hooked her legs around his waist.

It wasn't gentle and it wasn't tender. It was fast and raw. Unadorned, unapologetic sex.

And as far as Nathan was concerned, it was a hell of a lot better than arguing.

Sunlight glinted from the rifle of one of the men on guard duty near the entrance to the gravel pit. From her vantage point near the pit's edge, Kelly could see another one of Cooper Webb's men move through the brush on the far side. She should be accustomed to being around armed guards. God knew, they had been a fact of life at Stephan's estate. Still, firearms always made her nervous. She had to remind herself that these men had been well paid to be on her side.

Kelly jumped as a crow squawked from the grove of trees behind her. She looked around and spotted the bulky form of Pete Wysinski, the manager from

Cooper's old bar. He gave her a friendly wave and shuffled off. Kelly took a moment to steady her pulse—the sight of a man Pete's size would make anyone's heart skip a beat—then found a shady spot and sank down to sit on a patch of grass.

There was no shelter from the sun for the handful of men who worked on the floor of the pit. They moved through air that shimmered with heat. Nathan had discarded his shirt half an hour ago when it had become soaked with sweat. Even from up here, Kelly could see his skin was gleaming as he maneuvered a handcart down the ramp from the back of the eighteen-wheeler.

The handcart was piled with bread-box-size plastic packages. Cooper's men had drained the perc into a series of tanks that Pete had managed to borrow and had finished removing the heroin from the drums around noon. All that was left to do now was to transfer it to a less conspicuous vehicle.

Kelly saw Nathan pause to wipe the back of his hand over his forehead, and she felt a stirring of guilt for enjoying watching him work. Yet what woman wouldn't enjoy watching him? His body was magnificent. Each time he moved, his muscles flexed under sun-bronzed skin. The tan khakis he'd bought at the mall the day before rode low on his hips, providing a tempting view of the chiseled planes of his torso.

Only a few hours ago she'd had her legs around those hips, had felt the waistband of those khakis rub against her bare thighs...

She drew up her feet and wrapped her arms around her legs. Just thinking about what she and Nathan had done sent tingles skidding across her nerves.

Yet she didn't want to think about it. Making love

with Nathan was wonderful as long as she *didn't* think. For the first time in her life, she had learned what it felt like to have her body completely sated. The pleasure he had given her had let her escape, but she had known all along the respite had been temporary. This was reality. She had to keep her priorities straight.

She moved her gaze to the dump truck that was parked beside the eighteen-wheeler. As camouflage went, the vehicle was a good choice. It wasn't new— rust darkened its red paint in several places—but it wouldn't be old enough to attract attention on the road. It had been used to carry loads of sand or gravel, so it had sturdy sides and a tarp that could be unrolled to cover the load. Once the heroin was arranged in the bottom, it would be completely concealed.

Yes, the truck should work out fine. Just the thing for transporting a two-ton ransom payment.

She watched Nathan transfer the stack of packages from the handcart to the bed of the dump truck. They looked as harmless as bags of flour, but each one contained ten kilos of pure heroin, more than twenty-two pounds. One bag alone would bring a fortune on the street. There were more than a hundred and eighty bags.

The amount boggled her mind and turned her stomach. Yet she had been living off the proceeds of drugs like these for more than three years. She might have soothed her conscience by thinking she sang for a living, but the Starlight was Stephan's. The luxurious suite she'd lived in had belonged to him. All of Jamie's toys, his clothes, the equipment in his play yard and the books she read to him at bedtime had been purchased with drug money.

It was only natural that she'd worry the taint had

rubbed off. Could she really excuse the despicable things she'd done by saying they were for her son? The worst thing of all was her plan to use Nathan as a scapegoat.

Then again, he'd taken that particular piece of news rather well.

The bubble of laughter surprised her. She pressed her lips together to tamp it down. She didn't want to think about that, she reminded herself.

The grass rustled with a soft footfall. A moment later, Hayley's voice came from over her shoulder. "Now I see why you disappeared up here. This is some view."

Kelly glanced behind her. "It's also shady. I feel sorry for…" She almost said "the boys" the way Hayley had the day before, but she stopped herself. "For Nathan and Cooper."

"Darn, it looks as if they're almost done."

"What?"

"Too bad I didn't get here sooner." Hayley sat beside her, curling her legs to one side and tucking her skirt around her knees. "There's just something about a man when he's all hot and sweaty…" Her words trailed off on a sigh.

Kelly couldn't prevent her smile. Until now, she hadn't noticed that Cooper had stripped to the waist, too. He wore a snug pair of cutoff jeans, so he had more skin showing than Nathan.

Hayley's cheeks flushed pink as she watched Cooper move another load out of the trailer behind Nathan. Even though the Webbs had been married for almost two months, apparently the honeymoon wasn't over. "It's hard to imagine the dollar value of what they're handling," she said.

"It's the price of getting my son."

Hayley put her hand on her shoulder and squeezed lightly. "That's something else I can't imagine. This must be horrible for you."

"It's worse for Jamie."

"You'll have him back soon."

"Yes, thanks to Nathan and Cooper. I wish there was some way to repay you for all you're doing."

"Oh, don't get started on that." Hayley withdrew her hand. "These Payback guys have all the debts they can handle."

Kelly rested her cheek on her knees so she could study Hayley. Cooper's wife looked more like an angel today than ever, with the suffused sunlight on her blond hair and a smile on her face. Yet her husband had belonged to Payback, so he must have a criminal past like Nathan.

There had been so many other things to worry about, Kelly hadn't given much thought to Nathan's debt to Tony Monaco, but she should have. It was why Nathan had become involved with Stephan's organization in the first place. "Have you ever met Tony Monaco?" she asked.

Hayley shuddered delicately. "No. I don't think many people have."

"He must be a very kind man to have established an organization like Payback. It's wonderful how he helps people turn their lives around."

"I'm not sure about *kind,* Kelly. Tony can be ruthless with anyone who breaks their promise to him, but he does have a strong sense of fair play."

"Ruthless?"

"He was the heir apparent to a mob at one time."

Kelly shifted on the grass to face her. "And yet he runs a charity now."

Hayley lifted her eyebrows. "Is that what Nathan told you?"

She thought about it. "Not in those words. He told me that Tony gave him the help he needed to go straight."

"And did Nathan tell you how he had to pay that favor back?"

Kelly nodded. "That's why he needs to bring Stephan and his organization to justice. It's to even the score for the crimes of his past. He said that's the principle behind Payback."

"There's more to it than that."

"I know. It's about honor. Nathan's determined to keep his word."

"Ultimately, yes, it is about honor." She glanced at Cooper, her expression tender. "It's a way for a man to prove that he's put his past behind him so he can build a future."

"I can understand that. Maybe I should see if Tony will let me join."

Hayley whipped her gaze back to Kelly. "You don't need to do that. You're already taking steps to go straight. Don't risk what you can build in the future by making a deal with Tony."

"What risk would there be?"

"If you don't pay Tony back..." Hayley's words trailed off and her forehead furrowed.

"Don't stop now," Kelly said. "What happens if you don't pay him back?"

Hayley hesitated, then shook her head and rose to her feet. "I think you'd better ask Nathan."

Kelly turned back to the gravel pit, her gaze automatically finding the tall, sun-bronzed man in khakis. After this morning, she had thought there were no more secrets between them.

God, was there something *else* he hadn't told her?

Chapter 12

"Everything? What does that mean?"

"Just what I said. Everything I own. My company, my home, my cars, every painting on my walls, every stock in my portfolio and every cent in my bank accounts."

"But—"

"It's what we all agreed to when we joined Payback, Kelly." He closed the door and set the lock, then walked across the loft to the kitchen and opened the refrigerator. "If I renege on my deal with Tony, I leave the organization with exactly what I brought in. No more and no less."

She followed him. "How is that possible?"

"With Tony, anything's possible." His shirttails swung forward loosely as he leaned over to look into the fridge—he hadn't bothered to fasten the buttons after he'd put his shirt back on at the gravel pit. He took out a can of soda and held it out to her.

She shook her head. Her stomach was churning too much for her to think about adding anything to it. "I don't understand. Pack Leader is a legitimate company. Does Tony have part ownership or something? Can he force you out that way?"

"He doesn't have a legal claim on my company, but he doesn't need one." Nathan closed the fridge door and popped the tab on the soda. He took a long swallow, then pressed the cold can to his forehead. "He'll find a way to put Pack Leader out of business."

"How?"

"It wouldn't be that difficult. It might start out with a few trucks breaking down and the parts needed to repair them wouldn't be available. Some shipments might go to the wrong address or go missing altogether. After several months of that, customers would get scarce and the company would go into a downward spiral."

"Would he really do that?"

"Not personally. Tony gets other people to do that kind of work for him." Nathan took another drink and regarded her over the rim of the can. "I've done it myself when someone didn't pay their debt. It's all part of what it means to belong to Payback."

"What about the rest of your things? Your personal property and your investments? Are you saying he would get other Payback people to…steal everything?"

"Technically, it wouldn't be stealing. It would be closer to repossessing or foreclosing. Tony does bend the rules, but he prefers not to break them."

"My God." She sat on one of the stools beside the breakfast bar. Had she thought that Tony Monaco was charitable? He sounded ruthless, just as Hayley had said. No wonder she had warned Kelly to steer clear of him. And no wonder Nathan was so determined to pay his debt. "You'd truly be left with nothing?" she asked.

"Not nothing. Like I said, I'd leave Payback with what I brought in."

"What did you bring in?"

"Eighteen grand in cash, my favorite knife and my Harley." He drained the can and crushed it in his fist. "But all that is irrelevant, Kelly, because I intend to keep my promise. I just finished loading the bait that's going to put Volski away."

"I had no idea there was so much at stake for you," she murmured. "I thought the whole idea of bringing Stephan to justice was only a matter of honoring your word to a friend."

"Tony's not exactly a friend."

"Then how did you get mixed up with him?"

Nathan dropped the can on the counter and shrugged off his shirt. He used it to blot the back of his neck. "Are you sure you want to go into all of this now?"

No…what she'd really like to do was ogle his body. The loft had heated up over the course of the afternoon. With no blinds yet on the windows, the air-conditioning hadn't been able to keep up with the sunlight. Yet she knew it wasn't the temperature that was making her feel flushed. "Yes, unless you're in a hurry to take a shower."

He lifted one eyebrow. "Is that an invitation?"

It was more tempting than it should have been. She hooked her heels onto the rung of the stool and clasped her hands in her lap. "Nathan, you know so much about me. I'd like to know more about you."

"You already know more about me than anyone who knows me as Beliveau."

That was true, she realized. The people she had met at Pack Leader wouldn't have seen this side of Nathan. In a way, he had been living a lie for years, just as she had. A different kind of lie, though. The transformation from Rand to Beliveau was all good.

Yet the more time she spent with him, the less she thought of him as either one man or the other. Oh, this was confusing. "How did you meet Tony?"

He balled his shirt in his hands, then crossed his ankles and leaned back against the counter. "I made the mistake of stealing his car."

She pressed her fingers to her mouth. "You're kidding."

"At that time, I usually let my staff handle the acquisitions, but it was a fire-engine-red Ferrari, too good to pass up. I had no idea who owned it. If I had…" A corner of his mouth lifted in a half smile. "Well, I would have left it alone and we wouldn't be standing here now."

"Then maybe it wasn't really a mistake."

"It sure felt like one then. Tony tracked me down before the engine had cooled. When I realized who he was, I thought I was dead."

"So what happened?"

"He had a look at my operation and liked what he saw. He said if I went legit, I could do better than that, so he offered to get me a new name and bankroll my next business if I agreed to join Payback."

"That was your fresh start."

"Yes, that was it." His smile faded. "At first I thought I had made a bad deal. Going straight was damn hard work, and it didn't pay anywhere near as well as stealing cars."

"But you stuck it out."

"It felt good not to be looking over my shoulder all the time. It felt good to be able to look in a mirror, too."

"I've almost forgotten what that's like," she said.

"You'll get there, Kelly. Once all of this is over, you and Jamie can have a fresh start, too."

"Yes, we will."

He pushed away from the counter. "Where were you planning to go when you got away from Volski?"

The answer didn't come as quickly as it should have. She had planned what she would do when she got away for years, yet now that the end was within reach, she hadn't been thinking about it. "California. Maybe L.A. I was hoping that would be far enough so that Stephan wouldn't find me. I thought I could get work singing there." She met his eyes. "What about you, Nathan?"

"Me?"

"When this is over and you settle your debt with Tony, what will you do?"

"I'll go back to making money."

"What else will you do? I mean when you're not working?"

"I might go to a Bulls game or attend an auction if there's a piece of art that I want."

She hesitated. "Alone?"

"Is this your way of asking me about my love life?"

She slid off the stool. "If you don't want to answer, I'll understand."

He started toward her. "Why not? I asked you about yours."

"That was different. You were trying to be practical. I'm just curious."

"I'm not currently involved with anyone, Kelly. I seldom date, and I haven't had a serious relationship with a woman for years. I spend most of my time at my business."

That surprised her. She would have expected a man of Nathan's sexual appetite to be more...active. And it was also surprising how pleased she was by the fact that he wasn't. "Why is that?"

"I haven't met anyone I'd want to take time off for." He held his shirt by the cuffs and flipped it over a few times to twist it on itself, then stepped up to her so he could loop it behind her back. "And I've definitely never met a woman who fascinates me the way you do."

She placed her hands on his chest. His skin was hot and slightly sticky. She inhaled a whiff of soap from his morning shower mixed with a hint of dust from the gravel pit and the tang of male sweat. The scent was unexpectedly arousing. She tried to concentrate. "But you like the life you have, don't you?"

"Sure, who wouldn't? I've worked my tail off for it."

"Then why are you gambling everything you've worked for in order to help me?"

"Because you needed help."

"I've thought all along it was more than that. Now that you told me how much you're risking, I know it *has* to be more. Otherwise, it doesn't make sense."

He slid his shirt down until it rested behind her buttocks and used it to tug her closer. "Did I mention that you're gorgeous as well as fascinating? Those jeans are almost as sexy on you as that gold dress."

"You're not really seeing me."

"I will if you take off those jeans."

"Would you still think I was sexy if I didn't need your help?"

He frowned. "What are you getting at?"

The idea had been floating in the back of her mind for days. She hadn't set out to bring it up, but it seemed as if there was no comfort zone when it came to their conversations. No polite middle road. There hadn't been time. "Nathan, these circumstances are pushing all of your buttons. I think you're helping me as a way to make up for not being able to help your mother."

"My…" He dropped his shirt on the floor and backed away. He held up his palms. "What the hell does my mother have to do with you and me?"

"Think about it. I know I said my situation with Stephan was different from her relationship with your stepfather, but there are similarities, too. You must be identifying with Jamie. Why else would you go to such lengths to save him?"

He stared at her. "I admit I feel sympathy for your son, but—"

"And you want to rescue me. You see this," she said, pointing to the shadow of the bruise on her jaw. "You don't see me."

"You're wrong."

"Am I?"

"Hell, yes."

"What do you think is going on between us?"

"Damn good sex."

"If you were that interested in sex, you would have a wife or a steady girlfriend. You wouldn't be spending most of your time working."

He swept his fingers through his hair savagely. "Kelly, what we have going between us is the only simple thing in this entire situation. Why do you want to complicate it?"

"Because I'm tired of lies. I'm fed up with secrets. I want to be honest."

"I am being honest. Maybe you're the one who isn't."

"I've told you everything, Nathan."

"Have you?"

"Don't you believe me?"

"The way this conversation's heading, if I say I don't, you'll start telling me I have trust issues."

"You're entitled to them. You had good reason not to trust me when we met, but you probably have trouble trusting any woman. You were betrayed by your own mother."

"Geez, where is this coming from?"

"She should have protected her child. Deep down, you probably blame her for not defending you."

He swore and paced across the room. He moved stiffly, as if he were looking for something to kick. He glanced at the mattress where they had spent the night, then turned to face her. "Fine. You want the truth? Sure, I blamed her. When I was a kid, I resented the hell out of her for not leaving the son of a bitch who was abusing her and trying to abuse me, but I grew out of it. That's not the reason I haven't wanted to have a woman in my life."

"Then what is?"

"The women I met as Beliveau expected me to be only him. They saw the respectable rich guy in the shirt and tie who did all the right things. With you, I was able to show you the whole package, and it felt good, Kelly. I could let you see the ugly parts, those pieces that don't fit. I've got edges I'll never smooth off." He braced his feet apart and crossed his arms. "I thought you liked what you saw. Obviously I was wrong."

She moved toward him, responding to the hurt in his voice and his body language. "Nathan, I'm sorry. This has gone too far. I didn't mean—"

"Sure, you did. You said before that I've got a protectiveness thing going with you, so this must have been bothering you for a while. You're concerned that I'm only attracted to you because you need my help. Does that sum up your problem?"

Her throat felt too thick for speech. She nodded.

"This works both ways, Kelly. Instead of questioning my motives, try looking at your own."

Her steps faltered.

"Tell me. Are you only attracted to me because I'm helping you?"

The denial she wanted to give him wouldn't come.

Oh, God. Was the pull she felt toward Nathan genuine, or was he right? Did she see him as her Prince Charming, here to rescue her and whisk her into a fairy tale where dreams came true?

The pattern was familiar. It was how she had deluded herself with Stephan.

Damn, was she doing it again?

The silence went on too long. Nathan's gaze hardened, but it didn't harden fast enough to hide the flash of pain. "Or did it go further than that, Kelly?" he asked. "Was I wrong to think what we did last night was mutual?"

"What?"

"I believed that what I heard when you took me into your body and you moaned my name was real. But you know what I am and where I come from. You're worried about Volski's taint, so you'd have to be worried about mine."

"Nathan—"

"Yet for the sake of your son you'd be willing to put up with it, right? After all, I'm helping you, and you'd do anything for him. Is that what happened? Did you believe you had to pay for my favor by giving me yours?"

It took her a moment to grasp what he was saying. When she did, she wanted to weep. How could he possibly believe she'd felt coerced into making love?

How? She'd twice accused him of trying to do just that, when she'd asked him if he was trying to bid for her. Her insecurities about her own self-worth had managed to stir up his.

This just kept getting worse. The more they said, the more wounds they were opening up. Something fragile was shattering and she didn't know how to stop it. "Nathan, no. That's not what I felt."

"Then what do you feel, Kelly?"

The question shimmered in the air between them. She had done her best not to think about it, but she couldn't avoid it any longer.

What did she feel for Nathan? It was more than physical attraction, it had always been more. She had seen the whole package, and she *did* like what she saw. She loved what she saw.

Love? Her mind recoiled from the word. Oh, no. Whatever this was, it couldn't be love. It had to be need. Wishful thinking. It was because she was upset and looking for escape. It was because she'd seen the love that surrounded Hayley and Cooper and was still pathetic enough to long for the whole fairy tale herself....

Oh, God. She *was* doing it again.

Clouds had gathered with sunset, thick enough to block out the moon but not yet heavy enough to rain. They hung suspended along the horizon with lightning flickering through their bellies. The intermittent flashes only increased the charge that was building and prolonged the waiting for what was to come.

Kelly rolled to her back and watched another round of lightning dance across the ceiling. The weather outside was as frustrating as the atmosphere inside. She would have preferred the explosion of a storm to this waiting silence. Yes, as mindless as it would have been, as much as it wouldn't have solved anything, she would have preferred to end this afternoon's argument the way she and Nathan had ended the one this morning.

Damn good sex. That's what he'd said was going on between them. Maybe she should have left it at that. Why complicate things by digging for the truth?

She had gone too far, and as a result, she was lying on the mattress alone. Nathan was lying on the one beside her. He was on his back, a blanket tented over his up-drawn knees and one arm flung over his eyes. She could tell by his quiet breathing that he wasn't asleep.

She pictured herself turning over, reaching her hand across the gulf they had put between them and saying that she had one more secret to tell him, one last thing he needed to know.

But she was afraid. Lord, she was terrified.

What if this was another mistake?

Love. The word wouldn't go away, no matter how much she tried to drive it back. It was a feeling from her past, from the naive girl who had fled a broken heart and run away to the big city in search of her dreams. Love was what she'd longed for, but what did she know of it?

She and Marty had grown up next door to each other. They had known each other their entire lives. She had been certain she'd loved him, and it had been a mistake.

It had taken Stephan Volski months of charm to have her believe she loved him, and God, had *that* been wrong.

She had known Nathan for a week and a half.

Still, it had been an intense week and a half. The circumstances had forced them to skip the getting-acquainted part of their relationship. And somehow, the lies they had both been living had given them a bond no one else would understand. Their backgrounds had been different, yet strangely parallel, as if they fit together on more levels than merely the physical.

But this burning behind her eyes and the hollow pain in her chest couldn't be love. Not the storybook kind she'd sought before. This hurt.

Love shouldn't hurt, should it?

Yet the love she felt for Jamie wasn't the simple storybook kind, either, was it? It was tangled with guilt, regret and worry for his future. It was a constant ache in her heart.

And sometimes, it scared her, too.

The soft purr of Nathan's telephone made her pulse thud. She turned her head.

He'd left the phone beside his pillow. He put it to his ear without sitting up. "Yeah?" he said quietly.

She watched him, hardly daring to breathe. Lightning etched his profile in white. This time there was a distant hint of thunder, a rumble on the threshold of hearing, but not enough to release the tension. A minute crept by.

"All right," he said finally. "Thanks, Derek." He ended the connection and stretched his arm to set the phone on the floor.

"What did he want?" Kelly asked, propping herself up on her elbow. "Did he learn anything new?"

"He's not sure it's connected to Jamie, but he heard some of Volski's people were spotted in Lebanon."

"Oh, good Lord!" She sat up fast. "He took Jamie to the Middle East?"

"Lebanon, South Dakota," Nathan said. He curled into a sit-up and propped his forearms on his knees. "It might not have any connection to your son. Volski has customers in that area."

She shoved her hair behind her ears, her hands shaking. "Of course. The Canyon Brotherhood are based in South Dakota. I'd forgotten."

"I didn't mean to alarm you."

"It's fine. I want you to tell me what's going on, whether it's good news or bad."

"We'll get him back, Kelly." He looked at her. There was a lull in the lightning. In the darkness, she couldn't discern his expression, yet she could see his tension in the set of his shoulders. He seemed to be waiting, just like the storm.

"What is it?" she asked. "Is there something else about Jamie?"

"You were right this afternoon," he said. "One of the big reasons I want to help your son is because he reminds me of myself. Without someone to defend him, the things that happened to me could happen to him, and I want to do everything I can to get him back to you."

She twisted on her knees to face him. "I shouldn't have thrown that business about your mother at you. You didn't deserve to be ambushed like that."

"Why not? I've been pushing you all along, so it's natural that you would push back." He paused and rubbed the nape of his neck. "There was some truth in what you said about that, too. It still eats at me that I wasn't able to stop my stepfather from abusing my mother. Seeing your bruises reminded me of the way she used to look after he went on one of his drinking binges."

"You were only a child. You couldn't have done anything."

"Maybe. I'll never know for sure. It's possible that I am trying to help you as a way to make up for not being able to help her."

"I'm sorry for dredging it up. Those have to be painful memories."

"No, you had the right idea. It's better if we get things straight."

But they weren't straight, she thought. They were getting more confusing by the second. "Nathan..."

"And just to be sure there's no mistake, you need to know that I'm not expecting anything from you. Now or in the future. You're under no obligation to me."

"What do you mean?"

"I understand the world you've been living in, Kelly, because that's the kind of ugliness I came from. It's a world where people get used, and most relationships involve a victim."

And love is a tool, she thought, and sentiment is a weakness. Yes, he would know about the nightmare she'd been living. Their caution when it came to trusting people was another bond that they shared.

"So I want to make this clear," he said. "My help didn't come with any strings attached. Sleeping with me was never part of the deal."

She was thankful for the lull in the lightning. He wouldn't be able to see how her lips trembled. Even if she did extend her hand across the space between them, she probably wouldn't be able to reach him. The distance that separated them now was more than physical.

"No, it wasn't part of the deal, Nathan," she murmured. "Whatever emotional baggage we both brought into this, the sex we shared was mutual."

A charged silence crackled between them. Nathan exhaled hard. "It was incredible, Kelly," he said, his voice hoarse. "But we both know that's not why we're together. Your priority is your son."

"Yes."

"I accept that. You love him, and you'll do everything in your power to keep him safe." His eyes gleamed as he studied her in the darkness. "That's what you do when you love someone."

Why did she feel like crying? "Yes, it is."

He turned his head toward the window and cleared his throat. "Once Volski is arrested and you have Jamie back, the FBI will take care of you. Templar promised last week that you would have full immunity from any charges that might come up, and I mean to make sure she keeps her word. She'll get you into the witness protection program and relocate you where Volski won't be a threat." He hesitated. "That's still what you want, isn't it?"

She nodded. "We have to leave. We can't stay in Chicago. Stephan has a long reach, and even from prison he might try to get Jamie away from me if he knew where we were."

"I understand. It would be safest for Jamie if you both disappeared."

"Nathan, if Stephan finds out who you really are, he might want to retaliate against you. It might be better if you disappeared, too."

Another silence. This one lasted longer. "If I run,"

Nathan said finally, "I'll be giving up Pack Leader and everything I've worked for. I can't do that."

Kelly should have known that would be his response. She understood how much his new life meant to him. Running away had been the only choice for the child Nathan had once been, but it wouldn't be an option for the man Nathan was now. Like the wolf that was his talisman, like the warriors in his ancestry, he would fight for what was his.

God, she wanted to weep again. This was already sounding like a goodbye. "I'd like you to know that I appreciate everything you've done."

"I don't want your gratitude, Kelly."

Tell him!

But tell him what?

The phone rang again. Nathan snatched it from the floor and rose to his feet. He listened for a moment, then paced to the window. "It's under control, Tony."

Rain spattered the glass like a handful of tossed pebbles. The sky beyond flickered with white, silhouetting Nathan's tall, lean body. He had left his boxers on tonight, a mute acknowledgement of the distance between him and Kelly, but the rest of him was naked. He was as compelling to watch as the approaching storm.

Kelly hugged her knees to her chest as she listened to Nathan explain their revised plans to Tony. This was the wrong time to worry about her feelings; it was a ridiculous time to speculate about love. What was the point? If everything went according to plan tomorrow, she and Nathan would end up half a continent apart.

But if something went wrong…

She clamped her jaw hard to keep her teeth from chattering. She knew what Stephan was capable of.

What if he decided not to trade the heroin for Jamie? What if the FBI failed to arrest him? Tony would take away everything Nathan owned. The FBI would regard them as drug-smuggling fugitives and there would be nothing to keep Stephan from retaliating against both of them.

She would never see her baby again.

But if everything went right, she would never see Nathan again.

Oh, God. Just when she thought things couldn't get any worse, they did.

Chapter 13

Like anyone in the courier business, Nathan was well acquainted with this area of south Chicago—far more goods were moved through the Port of Chicago than through O'Hare Airport. Although they were still a few miles from the Lake Michigan shoreline, he could see the grid of lights from a tanker transfer station in the distance and the sheen of water in the canal between the warehouses to his left.

During daylight hours, the place was a hive of activity as cargo was unloaded from freighters and barges, but at night the action tapered off. There would be no casual passersby, no innocent eyewitnesses, and anyone who was around would know enough to mind their own business. It would be the ideal location for the meeting with Stephan Volski.

Nathan eased the dump truck to the side of the

road and took his hands from the wheel to wipe his
wet palms on his pants, trying to control a growing
sense of dread. He was no stranger to fear—he'd
grown up surrounded by it and had learned how to
cope with this kind of tension before he'd learned
how to read.

He'd been in worse spots before. When he'd been
running crack for the gang in Detroit, he'd faced the possibility of violent death on a daily basis. Later, when
he'd been boosting cars, one small miscalculation could
have landed him in prison. And still later, after he'd
come to Chicago and made the transformation to
Beliveau, his debt to Tony had hung over his head in a
constant reminder that he could lose it all.

Yet until now, he hadn't felt anything close to this
level of gut-churning cold.

He turned his head to look at Kelly. The rain of the
night before had lingered throughout the day, so she
wore the bulky Pack Leader windbreaker she'd used on
Friday. The blue-tinged light from the streetlight across
the road washed the color from her features but it failed
to dim the determination that shone from her face. The
love Kelly had for her son was as much a part of her as
the green in her eyes or the red in her hair.

She was hanging on by sheer willpower. Nathan
didn't need to see the dark circles that tinged the skin
beneath her eyes to realize she was nearing exhaustion.
Neither of them had slept much last night. They hadn't
slept much the night before that, either, but for an entirely different and far more pleasant reason. When it
came to her emotions, Kelly didn't do anything halfway.

If Nathan could turn back the clock, yesterday would
have ended differently, yet regrets were useless. If he let

himself get started on them, the number would be too long to list.

Still…the sex with Kelly had been unlike anything he'd experienced in his life. It had blown him away, just like her singing. He should have taken what she'd given him and have been happy with that, whatever her motives might have been.

Why should it matter to him, anyway? Why had he wanted to dig for the truth about her feelings? After tonight, their association would be over. She could start the new life she had planned, and Nathan could keep the life he had. It was what they both wanted, wasn't it?

Sure. Absolutely. This had been inevitable from the start. It was easier to be alone. As long as there was no one to care about, there was no one else to worry about, no one you had to trust, no one who could hurt you. It was a simple principle. It had worked for Nathan his entire adult life.

He had his priorities straight. He wasn't looking for a woman. And even if he was, it damn well wouldn't be this one.…

He'd tried telling himself the same thing more than a week ago.

Did he think if he repeated it often enough he might begin to believe it?

"Nathan?" Kelly asked. "Is something wrong?"

Hell, where should he start?

But this wasn't the time or the place for the discussion they needed to have. "No, everything's fine, Kelly. We're right on schedule." Nathan dug his phone out of his pocket and keyed in Templar's number.

The FBI agent's voice was finely honed steel, sounding even sharper than it had when he'd called her this afternoon. "Where are you now, Mr. Beliveau?"

"We're in south Chicago, about two miles from the meeting site." He told her the names of the nearest cross streets as he took stock of his surroundings, looking for a more private place to park.

"Stay there. I have a unit five minutes away from your location. They'll fit you and Miss Jennings with wires and vests and brief you on the route to follow to the rendezvous."

He was glad Templar didn't waste time with more recriminations. She'd been livid when she had learned Volski's child would be involved in the sting, but she'd had to acknowledge it was too late to change their plans now.

"There's an empty lot northeast of the intersection," Nathan said. "We'll wait for them there."

"You'd better," Templar snapped. "If you fail to keep your agreement this time, I intend to pursue you to the full extent of the law."

"Understood." Nathan terminated the connection and put the truck back in gear to pull off the street. Four minutes later, a dark blue panel van turned into the lot and came to a stop behind him.

At any other time, he would have marveled at the fact that he was cooperating with the authorities. Less than a week ago, he'd dragged his heels about merely making a phone call, yet now he was not only on the same side as the law, he was going to make sure they enforced it. There was a lot more at stake now than keeping his promise to Tony.

Yet Nathan knew the impending confrontation with Stephan Volski wasn't what was making his palms sweat and his heart pound. No, the fear that was seeping into his bones was from something else entirely.

It was because what he felt for Kelly scared the hell out of him.

* * *

Kelly fought the urge to scratch at the microphone that was fastened inside her blouse. The FBI agents who had given it to her had cautioned her not to draw attention to it in any way. This was how they would confirm when Jamie was safe and the heroin had changed hands so they would know when to move in. But she doubted if whoever was listening on the other end would be able to hear anything over the thud of her heart, the chattering of her teeth and the rumbling of the truck's engine. She clamped her jaw and leaned forward on the seat, peering into the darkness as Nathan followed the length of the pier.

The waterfront along this stretch of the Lake Michigan shoreline was a maze of warehouses and docks. Moored freighters loomed in the darkness beside the pier, their hulls rising like sloping steel walls. A network of girders and giant cranes that would be used to unload them towered overhead. Among all these massive ships and monstrous equipment, a lone dump truck would hardly be noticed, but Kelly knew their progress was being monitored. There were plenty of places for the FBI to conceal themselves. Simply because she couldn't see anyone didn't mean they weren't there.

But where was Stephan? And where was Jamie? Shouldn't she be able to tell if he was near?

Nathan turned onto a narrow pier at right angles from the last one. Only one ship was moored alongside here. It took up the entire length of the dock. Beyond it was only the blackness of the lake. Nathan drove to the end and executed a series of tight maneuvers to reverse the direction of the truck. Once they were facing the way they had come, he backed to the end of the pier, set the brakes and shut off the engine.

Kelly clasped her hands in her lap and inhaled hard through her nose. The smell of water and diesel fumes rolled through the open window, along with the sound of waves lapping against the hull of the ship beside them. "What time is it?" she asked.

Nathan checked his watch. "11:57."

"I can't believe this is actually happening," she said. "It seems so unreal."

"I see headlights."

She leaned forward eagerly, her forehead bumping the windshield. He was right. Among the lights that shone from the warehouses and transit sheds along the shore, two sets moved. "Oh, God," she whispered. "Could that be them?"

The lights drew nearer. Three minutes later, two vehicles—a sleek black limousine followed by a boxy black Hummer—passed beneath the glow of a lighted sign in front of a warehouse. While the Hummer stopped at the foot of the pier, the limo turned and drove directly toward them.

The plan was to trade vehicles. Stephan and his men would leave with the truck, while Kelly and Nathan would take the limo with Jamie. She reached for the door handle but Nathan grasped her arm to stop her.

"We have to wait inside until they come to a full stop and get out," he said. "Otherwise, Templar's people can't provide us with cover. That vest they gave you might be bulletproof, but the rest of you isn't."

She knew that. The agents had cautioned her about not exposing herself unnecessarily. She glanced at the ship that rose on her right. FBI snipers would be positioned out of sight along the deck. They had strict orders not to shoot if there was even a remote risk of a bullet hitting Jamie.

She squinted toward the headlights of the parked Hummer. The vehicle was unfamiliar—Stephan had probably acquired it to replace the Navigator that Nathan had totalled when he'd hit it with the semi. It would be filled with Stephan's guards, and they would be packing as much firepower as the FBI.

She was grateful that Stephan was paranoid enough to use an armored limo.

But did they have to drive so slowly? She folded her arms over her breasts and rocked back and forth, as if she could will the limo to move faster.

Was her baby in there? Was he awake? Was he frightened?

The vehicle came to a stop when it was ten yards away. For a moment nothing was visible except the twin glare of its headlights, but then Nathan switched on the spotlight that was mounted on the side of the truck and the scene was illuminated like day. Alex Almari emerged from the driver's side and went to open the rear doors.

Kelly held her breath. She knew it was too soon. Still, she couldn't stop the whimper of disappointment when she saw Dimitri Petrovich and then Stephan step out of the limo empty-handed.

"Okay," Nathan murmured, opening his door. "Stay close to me, Kelly. It's almost over."

Her hands shook so badly, she had trouble getting her door open. Nathan rounded the truck and helped her climb down, then guided her to stand by the bumper and took up a position slightly in front of her.

Stephan strode to the front of the limo. The legs of his pale gray trousers and the ends of the matching suit jacket flapped in the breeze from the lake. In the flood-light his hair was bleached silver and his skin as pale as paper, except for the dark lines of scabs that marred his left cheek. "Where is my merchandise, Rand?" he called.

Nathan tipped his head behind him. "In the dump box."

"Show me proof."

"I will, as soon as you show me the child."

Yes, Kelly thought. Oh, yes. Dear God, let her baby be here…let him be all right.

Stephan smoothed his hand over his tie to hold it down in the breeze. "He is fatigued from the trip and is sleeping. I do not wish to disturb him yet."

"Disturb him," Nathan said. "His mother won't mind. Otherwise, my next stop will be your customers."

Stephan snapped his fingers at Alex. The hulking en-forcer-turned-chauffeur stepped around Dimitri and leaned into the open door of the limo. A minute later he straightened up and turned toward them. In his arms he held a tiny figure wrapped in a light blue blanket.

Kelly lunged forward.

Before she could take more than a step, Nathan grabbed her by the waist and hauled her back. "I'm sorry, Kelly," he said. "Not yet."

She knew he was right. She had to wait until the drugs changed hands so the FBI could arrest Stephan, yet she trembled with the need to move. Jamie was here, and she yearned to go to him with every fiber of her being. She wanted to touch him, to see his smile and stroke his hair, to smell the sweet little-boy scent that came from his skin, but he was too far away. With the blanket bunched at his shoulders, she couldn't even see his face.

Somehow, she kept her protest inside. All the practice she'd had keeping silent over the past three years was good for something. Thank God, he was sleeping. There was a chance he might not remember this when he got older. She could only hope that whatever he'd endured until now wouldn't come back to haunt him.

"Now I will see your proof, Rand," Stephan said.

Nathan took Kelly's hand, guided her to the hood of the truck and waited until she steadied herself before he stepped back. "Only a few more minutes," he said. "Can you make it?"

She bit her lip and nodded.

"Talk to the bitch on your own time," Stephan said. "I don't have all night."

Kelly could see Nathan tense. He'd been on edge all day, but the strain that hummed through his frame now was worse. No wonder. Everything he owned was riding on the success of this exchange.

Nathan moved to the rear of the truck cab and worked the mechanism to roll up the tarp that concealed the load. Once it was tied off, he gestured to the narrow metal ladder that was bolted to the front edge of the dump box. "Be my guest, Volski. It's all there. You're welcome to climb up and count it."

Kelly fought to keep her gaze away from the ship beside them. Oh, could it be this easy? If the FBI could catch Stephan actually surrounded by his heroin…

Stephan didn't move. He cocked his thumb at Dimitri. "Take a look and tell me what you see. I want an accurate count."

It seemed to take forever for the lanky Dimitri to climb the ladder. He disappeared over the top edge of the box, and once again, Kelly found herself rocking back and forth, subconsciously urging him to move faster. She returned her gaze to Jamie. He hadn't stirred. Alex cradled him awkwardly, as if he were holding an armload of firewood.

"You appear to be as eager to conclude our business as I am, Kelly."

At Stephan's comment, she shifted her gaze. The damage she had done to his face with her nails appeared deep enough to scar, but she realized she had no remorse. She made no effort to veil the revulsion she felt at his presence. Only another few minutes, and he would be out of her life forever.

Stephan smirked. "Could it be you're in a hurry because you don't want to allow your new friend any time to realize what a poor bargain he has made?"

"Shut up, Volski," Nathan said.

"He'll tire of you as fast as I did, Kelly. You don't have what it takes to please a man."

She wouldn't give him the satisfaction of letting him see how his words hurt. "You're not a man, Stephan. You're a monster."

"Better that than a sentimental fool." He looked at Nathan. "Has she declared that she loves you yet, Rand? That would be her next ploy."

"Try not to make yourself a bigger ass than you already are, Volski," Nathan said. "Is this what you want your son to hear?"

"It is high time the boy learns the way of the world. His mother is too soft. He needs the influence of a real man." Stephan's smirk widened. "How unfortunate that you do not fit that requirement, Rand."

"On second thought, even you're not that big an ass," Nathan said. "You're saying all this to distract us. I wonder why."

Even across the distance that separated them, Kelly couldn't mistake the shrewdness on Stephan's face. Nathan was right. Stephan was deliberately trying to distract them, but from what?

She returned her gaze to Jamie. He was a good sleeper, but it was strange that he still hadn't stirred in spite of the raised voices around him....

Her pulse thumped. "Alex," she called. "Take the blanket away from Jamie's face."

Alex didn't move. He looked at Stephan.

"You do not give directions to my men, Kelly," Stephan said. "You should know by now that they obey only me."

Kelly swayed forward, her blood turning to ice. "Jamie?" she called. "Baby? It's Mommy."

There was no trace of movement beneath the blue blanket, no sleepy voice, no child's sigh. *No sign of life.*

"It's all there, Mr. Volski," Dimitri called from behind her. He moved past, one of the plastic packages of heroin held in his hands. "One hundred and eighty-two bags, including this one."

"Excellent," Stephan said. "Bring that one here. I wish to test it."

Kelly barely registered the men's voices. Panic engulfed her. No. Dear God, it couldn't be, but he was so still... "Jamie, wake up!" she shouted. *"Jamie!"*

For the second time, Nathan caught her before she could run forward. She struggled to free herself, lashing out with her elbows and her heels but he hung on in spite of her blows. "Get in the truck, Kelly," he ordered. "Now."

She shook her head, her vision blurring. "Something's wrong with Jamie. He's not waking up. I have to—"

Nathan lifted her from her feet and pivoted toward

the passenger door of the dump truck. "That's not Jamie," he said, tossing her up to the seat. "The bastard's double-crossing us. Don't move until we have the child. Did you hear me? Nobody move."

The urgency in his words penetrated her panic. *Not Jamie. Double-cross.* It was a trick.

Yes, of course. It had to be. Stephan wouldn't allow Alex to hold Jamie—the man had endangered his son. Stephan wouldn't give up one of his prized possessions this easily, either. When had he ever told the truth?

It took no more than a heartbeat for Kelly to process the facts. Yet before she had, she saw Dimitri throw aside the package of heroin he carried and draw a gun.

Nathan dropped into a crouch, rolled to one side and came up with his switchblade. In a swift blur of motion, he flicked his wrist forward. The knife arced through the air and sank into the back of Dimitri's hand, the blade piercing straight through his palm.

The gun flew out of his grip and disappeared over the edge of the dock as Dimitri's high-pitched scream echoed from the hull of the ship. The ship with the FBI agents. But there was no sign of a sniper, no crackle of a bullhorn, no sign that anyone was there.

Don't move until we have the child. Did you hear me? Nobody move. Nathan's words had been meant for the FBI, Kelly realized. He was telling them to hold their fire.

Dimitri collapsed to his knees and cradled his hand to his chest, his scream tapering off to a series of moans. Blood ran down his arm and dripped from his elbow.

Stephan whirled on Alex. "Imbecile! Where's your gun?"

Alex reached into his jacket awkwardly with his left

hand, losing his grip on the bundle he held. A red velvet bolster, like the ones on the sofa outside her and Jamie's suite, tumbled out of the blanket and rolled across the dock, coming to rest against the limo's front wheel.

Nathan dived for the truck and climbed into the driver's seat. "Hold your position, Templar," he said, pitching his voice low so it wouldn't carry beyond the truck cab. "Volski doesn't have the dope yet. He didn't touch that sample Petrovich dropped. You've got nothing on him."

Kelly looked from the white plastic package of heroin to the blood that was dripping from Dimitri, then focused on the red bolster. She started to shake. "Where is he?" she whispered. "Where—"

"Hang on, Kelly." Nathan started the engine and reached for the hydraulic controls. "I'll get him for you."

There was a clunk from the back of the truck. A vibration traveled through the floorboards beneath her feet. She glimpsed movement in the rearview mirror that was set outside the door. With disbelief, she realized the dump box was tilting. "Nathan, what are you doing?"

"Negotiating."

Stephan looked at the truck, his eyes rounding. "Rand!" he yelled. "Stop!"

There was a gritty, slithering sound as the load behind them shifted. The plastic packages of heroin were sliding toward the tailgate.

Stephan held up his palms. "Let's not be so hasty, Rand. We're businessmen. We can come to an agreement."

Nathan let the angle of the dump box increase for another few seconds, then froze it where it was. He reached for Kelly's hand and placed it over the controls. "Press here to activate it again," he instructed. "We only have a few more degrees to play with, so don't let it go for more than five seconds."

"What—"

"Trust me." He squeezed her fingers and climbed down from the truck.

She inhaled on a sob. Trust him? There was no question that she did. She would trust Nathan with her life. With her son's life.

"You know what I want," Nathan called to Stephan. "Our agreement was for Kelly Jennings's child, not for a damn pillow."

Stephan spread his arms. "It was a misunderstanding."

"Prove it. Tell Alex to throw the gun in the lake."

Stephan's gaze darted toward Dimitri, who was curled into a fetal position, his moans continuing unabated. He scowled and barked an order in Russian over his shoulder at Alex. The man complied immediately, lobbing the gun that he'd just drawn over the side of the pier.

"Where's the boy?" Nathan asked.

"You must have patience," Stephan said. "These things take time."

"If you don't bring him here in the next five seconds, Kelly's going to dump your merchandise into the lake."

"You're bluffing. She wouldn't do that."

"You're already wearing a souvenir of the last time you got between her and her son. You don't want to push her again."

Stephan moved his gaze to the truck.

Kelly hit the switch Nathan had shown her and started to count. Metal groaned as the front of the dump box inched higher.

"All right!" Stephan shouted. "He's in the Hummer."

Kelly whipped her gaze to the headlights at the foot of the pier. Two seconds. Three.

Stephan took his phone from his jacket and crammed it against his ear. "Bring the boy here, now. *Now!*"

Four seconds. The headlights started moving toward them. Kelly took her hand from the switch.

The hum of the hydraulics didn't stop. She twisted to look behind her. The dump box continued to rise.

"Kelly!" Stephan shouted. "The boy's almost here, I swear it. Stop!"

The truck shuddered with a series of slaps as a hundred and eighty-one ten-kilo bags tumbled downhill. There was a grating creak from the very back. Kelly pictured the tailgate swinging open.

No, she thought frantically. The heroin was their evidence. Stephan had to take possession of it. Without that, the sting wouldn't work. She tried the controls again, but nothing changed. Six seconds. Seven.

"You stupid bitch!" Stephan dropped his phone, ran to the side of the truck and yanked open the door. "Stop or it will all be ruined."

Before he could put his foot on the step, Nathan grabbed him by his collar and flung him aside.

More headlights appeared from the darkness as vehicles converged on the pier, blocking the only way out. Floodlights switched on from the deck of the freighter. The rhythmic thump of a helicopter swelled overhead. Templar must have given the order to move in.

Yet despite the noise, Kelly was able to hear a splash.

Stephan shrieked, racing toward the back of the truck, his arms outstretched as if he meant to catch the falling packages.

Nathan climbed into the truck and slid behind the wheel.

"It's stuck, Nathan," she said. "I can't make it stop!
I'm sorry."

He looked at her, his gaze fierce. "I'm not."

"What?"

"Sorry." He didn't reach for the hydraulic controls.
Instead, he put the truck into gear, released the brakes
and drove forward.

Only a fraction of the heroin fell into the lake.

The remainder of the two tons fell directly on
Stephan Volski.

Chapter 14

Sirens echoed across the water as red lights flashed along the pier. A helicopter hovered overhead, its spotlight pinning the black Hummer as it was quickly overtaken by a trio of dark sedans. FBI agents poured out of the cars, taking cover behind the open doors as they pointed their weapons at the Hummer.

"No!" Kelly screamed. She leapt from the truck. "Don't shoot! My baby's in there!"

Nathan shut off the engine and sprinted after Kelly. "Damn it, Templar, make sure your people hold their fire!"

"Jamie!" Kelly called, her voice breaking. "Jamie!"

More agents were running toward them. Two men managed to intercept Kelly before she could go past the parked limo. She fought to break free, her lips curled into an expression that verged on a snarl.

"Kelly, it's okay," Nathan said. He caught her hands

before she could hit the agents again. "They're on our side. They want to make sure he's safe."

Kelly twisted her head to keep the Hummer in sight. "It's taking so long. Don't they know how scared he must be? He's only three!"

"We know everything, ma'am." The agent on her left stepped back and looked at Nathan. He pressed a finger to the receiver that was nestled in his ear and paused as if listening to instructions. "Mr. Beliveau, we need you to come with us."

"Not yet," Nathan said. He clamped one arm around Kelly's shoulders, slid his free hand inside her collar and ripped free the microphone that was under her blouse. He got rid of his own and shoved them at the agent. "Kelly, breathe," he said. "It's all right."

She clutched his wrist, her lips moving in what sounded like a prayer.

Several men ran past them, weapons drawn. From the corner of his eye, Nathan saw Alex Almari being frisked and handcuffed. Dimitri lay motionless, probably passed out from the pain. A few sacks of heroin had split open when they'd hit the dock, spilling clouds of white powder. Agents converged on the heap at the back of the dump truck and started pulling aside the packages. There was no haste to their movements—they had to realize there was little chance of recovering Volski alive.

"This is the FBI." A woman's voice blared through a bullhorn. "You are surrounded. Step out of the vehicle with your hands up."

They were the words Nathan had once dreaded hearing. There was still a part of him that always would, but right now they were as sweet as music. He looped his other arm around Kelly and waited.

One by one, the doors of the Hummer swung open. Volski's men climbed out, their hands empty and raised over their heads. Agents took charge quickly, herding the men aside and having them lie facedown on the dock. Four other agents closed in on the vehicle and cautiously looked inside. "Clear!" one shouted.

A plump, dark-haired woman emerged. Nathan felt a flood of relief as he recognized her. It was Gloria Hahn, Jamie's nanny. A split second later, he heard a child's cry. "Mommy!"

Kelly exploded from Nathan's arms. He didn't dream of stopping her. Neither did the FBI agents who surrounded them. She flew across the distance to the Hummer, her arms pumping, her hair streaming behind her. She reached the rear door on the passenger side just as a tiny figure scrambled over the seat and fell into her arms.

The helicopter still chugged overhead. An ambulance siren whooped in the distance. The scene bustled with voices and the crackle of radios as the FBI team continued to do their jobs. Yet a circle of calm settled around Kelly and her son.

She turned in the spotlight from the helicopter, her arms locked around her child, her eyes closed and her cheeks glistening. Jamie clung to his mother just as tightly, his body shuddering with sobs. Neither spoke. There would be time for that later. She sank to her knees and pressed her nose to his hair.

Nathan's eyes filled. He heard more than one agent clear their throat. In spite of the ugliness that surrounded them, they were witnessing love at its purest. Total and unconditional. It was a sight no one would forget.

"Mr. Beliveau." Someone touched his elbow. "Special Agent Templar wants to speak with you."

He blinked. Kelly was stroking Jamie's back, running her hands over his body as if she had to reassure herself he was really there. "Miss Jennings's son should be checked by a doctor," Nathan said. "Make sure he's all right."

"Yes, sir. We'll handle it."

"She shouldn't be left alone. She's been through hell. Do you have a counselor?"

"I assure you, we know how to deal with this kind of situation."

"Make sure Volski's men can't get loose. They—"

"Mr. Beliveau, it's over." The grip on his elbow firmed. "Come this way, please."

Nathan took one last look at Kelly. She was going to be all right. She had what she wanted.

But this wasn't over. Not by a long shot.

Kelly leaned the back of her head against the wall, her hand smoothing Jamie's hair. He was curled up beside her on the couch, his head in her lap as he slept. They had spent what was left of the night being passed from one official to another, first at the harbor, then at the Chicago headquarters of the FBI. She could see by the light that was filtering through the Venetian blinds on the office window that dawn was breaking, yet apart from Jamie, no one here had seemed to sleep.

Sandra Templar sat behind her desk, her head bent over the file that was open in front of her. Everything about her projected efficiency, from her short, salt-and-pepper hair to her no-nonsense tweed suit. With her good bone structure and firm features, her age was difficult to judge for sure—Kelly guessed she was in her midforties. There were no family pictures in her office, no clues to the personal life of the woman behind the badge, yet her tone had been gently compassionate as she had gone over the events of the previous night.

This was the final interview. Once they were finished here, Agent Templar had promised her she would be at liberty to leave.

The freedom was going to take a while to get used to. Kelly had once heard a story about a caged animal that had been set free, only to continue pacing the imaginary confines of its cage. In its mind, it was still trapped.

But Kelly knew she was free to go wherever she chose. Nothing was stopping her from taking her son and going anywhere in the world. There were no more guards to watch her every move. No more locked gates. Stephan was dead. In a stroke of poetic justice, he had been killed by his own dope.

In spite of the misery he had caused, she felt a stirring of sympathy for him. He couldn't have been born the way he was. Once, he must have been as innocent and full of promise as his son. Something along the way had warped him into choosing the path he had. He hadn't been able to see beyond his greed. While he'd been ruthlessly pursuing wealth and power, he'd never realized that he could have had the most precious thing on earth.

She rested her hand on Jamie's back, letting it ride with the gentle rise and fall of his breathing. Precious. Yes, that's what love was. Something to be cherished and nurtured. Something that endured forever and for always. She looked at her son and tears sprang to her eyes. She let them trail down her cheeks unheeded. They were good tears, cleansing tears.

Templar made a note on one of the papers in the file, put down her pen and looked up. "I'm afraid I can't allow you access to your belongings until my team finishes processing the Volski estate," she said. "I must warn you, some items could be confiscated as the proceeds of crime."

Kelly thought of the fortune in gowns Stephan had provided for her, the closets filled with shoes and designer handbags and the everyday wardrobe that was worth more than her parents had earned in their entire working lives. "I don't want any of it," she said. "All I had when I met Stephan was a suitcase of clothes from the Maple Ridge Walmart and sixty-two dollars in a straw purse." She smiled, thinking of what Nathan had told her about Payback. "I'd like to say that I'll leave with no more than I brought in, but I have to be practical. Jamie's going to need more than what he's wearing."

Templar nodded. "That won't be a problem. Miss Hahn provided us with the bag of clothes she had packed for your son before they had returned to Chicago. I'll arrange for you to pick it up downstairs."

Kelly wiped her cheeks. She had learned from Gloria that Stephan hadn't sent Jamie to his family in Russia after all. Instead, Jamie had been taken to the fortified compound of the Canyon Brotherhood—that was why some of Stephan's people had been in South Dakota. Stephan had meant to begin Jamie's "training" by having him raised among an outlawed militia group.

The horror of what might have happened to her baby under the influence of the Brotherhood was still too raw for her to think about. She would need to heal a bit more before she would be able to deal with that.

"Thank you," Kelly said. "Does this mean we're free to go?"

"In a moment." Agent Templar folded her hands on the desk. "I pride myself on keeping my word, Miss Jennings. I had agreed to grant you complete immunity and to relocate you and your son in the witness protection program. However, the circumstances have changed."

Kelly leaned forward quickly. "What do you mean?"

"Don't be alarmed. Your immunity is not affected. I'm merely tying up loose ends." Templar's lips softened in a brief smile. "Now that Stephan Volski is dead, I'm presuming that you no longer feel it necessary to relocate. Therefore I haven't yet started the paperwork that would put you in the program, but I did give my word."

Kelly laughed softly. "I don't want to run. There isn't any reason…" Her laughter died as she glanced around the office. Oh, how could she have forgotten? "Agent Templar, Stephan has someone on his payroll here. I don't know who it is, but—"

"Mr. Beliveau alerted me to this problem last week, Miss Jennings, and we've already flushed the individual out. He'll be facing a long list of charges."

"But Nathan won't, will he?"

"No, he won't," the woman confirmed. "We've determined that justice would not be served by prosecuting Mr. Beliveau for his actions during this affair. And as you know, your immunity doesn't depend on your testimony, but if you should choose to volunteer to tell us what you know, we would very much appreciate it. It will take us months to sort through the Volski organization."

"I'll give you whatever information I can."

"Then you're planning to stay in Chicago?"

"Absolutely." She pushed her hair behind her ears and looked for her jacket. "Is Mr. Beliveau still here?"

"Excuse me?"

"Here in the building. I heard he was being questioned."

"I'm afraid he left several hours ago."

Kelly tried to tell herself not to feel disappointed. She and Nathan had never discussed a future together. It hadn't seemed possible. She hadn't told him how she felt, so why would he hang around an FBI office to wait for her? She knew he didn't like cops, and she realized he had a life he was eager to get back to.

Maybe he wouldn't want to be burdened by a woman and a child, anyway. He had so many painful ghosts from his past, he might not be prepared to keep her and Jamie in his life....

She jerked her thoughts to a halt. What on earth was she doing? Pacing her imaginary cage?

There were other aspects of her new freedom that she'd better start getting used to. Everything had changed. She didn't have to hide her emotions, and she no longer needed to be afraid to trust her feelings.

And after everything she and Nathan had shared, there was no way in hell she was going to let him slip away, no matter what kind of issues they had yet to sort through. "Agent Templar?"

"Yes, Miss Jennings?"

She slipped her hand under Jamie's cheek so she could get to her feet, then picked him up from the couch. "Could you loan me cab fare?"

By the time Kelly reached the sidewalk, sunshine was tinting the tops of the buildings with gold. A street sweeper hummed past, its bristles gritting against the pavement. No one else was in sight, and for a moment Kelly savored the early-morning feel of the city. It was truly a time of new beginnings and fresh starts.

A car turned the corner, its wheels splashing along

the puddle the street sweeper had left. With the bag of Jamie's clothes hooked on her elbow, Kelly hitched her sleeping son against her shoulder and was about to start toward the curb when she realized the car wasn't the taxi she had called but a sleek, silver Jaguar sedan. She looked past it, waiting for it to go by.

It pulled to a stop in front of her. The driver's door opened and Nathan got out. "Good morning, Kelly."

The sight of him took her breath away. His hair was damp, his cheeks smooth from a fresh shave and a clean white shirt stretched across his wide shoulders. On top of that, he was smiling. She had once thought that his smile transformed his face. She'd been wrong. His smile only revealed what was always there: a man whose real handsomeness lay on the inside.

He popped open the trunk and rounded the car to reach for the bag that hung from her arm. "Going somewhere?"

He smelled so good, she wanted to lean into him and open her mouth against his neck and taste that dip at the base of his throat. "The airport," she said, shifting her hold on Jamie so Nathan could take the bag.

Nathan paused with the bag in his hand. "The airport? Why? You're not still planning to go to California, are you?"

"No, I was going to ask you for a job. I heard you had connections. You didn't tell me your phone number or where you live, but I do know where you work so..."

His smile grew. "You were coming to find me."

She felt a bubble of happiness rise in her chest. It felt great to tell the truth. "You bet. Where have you been?"

"Shopping."

"It's barely dawn. Nothing's open."

He winked. "That's why it took me so long." He

flung the bag into the trunk, closed the lid and returned. He touched his fingertips to Jamie's curls, then moved his hand to her cheek. "I wanted to be here when you finished with Templar."

"Why?"

"Because I have a confession to make, Kelly." He stroked the corner of her mouth with his thumb. "I lied."

She knew by his touch and by the warmth in his gaze that this was one lie she wouldn't mind hearing. She still trusted him, not only with her life but with her heart. "Again?"

"I said there were no strings, but there are. There's a connection between us that isn't going to break, no matter where you go."

Her pulse tripped. Oh, there was so much she wanted to tell him, and she didn't want to wait a minute longer. "Nathan, I—"

"Mommy?" With the impeccable timing typical of young children, Jamie chose that moment to wake up. He rubbed his forehead against her shoulder. "Mommy, I'm thirsty."

"I'll get you some juice in a little while, okay?"

Nathan dipped his head. "Good morning, Jamie."

Jamie yawned, his thumb inching toward his mouth. He studied Nathan solemnly but didn't respond.

Kelly rubbed Jamie's back. After what her son had been through, it was understandable that he would be subdued and more cautious than he used to be. The trauma counselor who had spoken with her earlier had said it was to be expected, but Jamie was in good health and with his mother's support, he should recover.

"How's he doing?" Nathan asked quietly.

"He'll be fine."

"I've got something in here that might help." Nathan turned to the car and opened the rear door.

He had indeed been shopping, Kelly saw. The back-seat was crammed with colorful bags from every children's store in Chicago. Clothes, baseballs and stuffed toys spilled onto the floor. In the middle of it all was a brand-new child safety seat. Somehow, he must have convinced the store managers to open just for him. "Nathan, this is so generous."

"No, this stuff isn't what I meant." He leaned inside and dug through the pile. From beneath an enormous plush teddy bear, he pulled out a worn toy rabbit. "Here."

At the sight of his favorite toy, Jamie squirmed in her arms. He stretched out his hands, his face alight. "Bunny!"

Kelly's vision blurred with yet another rush of tears, so she didn't actually see Nathan hand the toy to her son. But she did feel Jamie's body relax as he cuddled the rabbit to his cheek. "How did you get this?" she asked.

"Connections."

"What…"

"I talked some of Templar's people into looking for it."

"Thank you. That was exactly what he needed."

"I don't want your gratitude, Kelly."

He'd said that once before. This time, she *was* going to tell him. "Nathan…"

He leaned over and kissed away her tears before they could fall, then slipped his arms around her back, enveloping both her and her son in his embrace. "Kelly, for the past six hours I've been trying to think of the right way to say this. Now that you're here, I can't remember anything."

"Nathan, I—"

"If anyone deserves the whole fairy tale, it's you, but we're both tired, and we're on a public sidewalk in front of a building filled with feds, so I'm going to keep it simple." He looked at Jamie, then met her gaze squarely. "You're mine. You're part of me. I feel you inside my heart the same way you must feel your son. I'm not sure what love is, but that's the only word that comes to mind."

She laid her hand on his chest. Yes, he was here and was actually saying these things. This wasn't wishful thinking or a fairy tale. He was a real man, with faults and scars and complexities she hadn't begun to discover. "I know what it is, Nathan, because I feel the same thing."

Beneath her palm, his heart was pounding. "I love you, Kelly."

"I love you, too, Nathan."

The street sweeper came back, making a circuit on the other side of the street. A taxi pulled up in front of Nathan's car and beeped its horn.

As far as Kelly was concerned, the ordinary, everyday noises made the perfect backdrop to the extraordinary sound of a dream coming true.

Nathan smiled and put his mouth next to her ear as the sweeper drew closer. "There's something else I've been thinking about for the past six hours, Kelly."

Public sidewalk or not, she shuddered in delight at the brush of his lips on her earlobe. "Oh?"

"But unless we want to be arrested, before we get to that part, I'd better take you home."

Epilogue

Nathan carried the cushions back to the couch, wincing when his foot came down on another metal toy car. The clean, airy lines of his penthouse had all but disappeared beneath the drifts of toys and children's clothes. There were tiny palm prints all over the windows and crayon marks on the floor. Cookie crumbs and puddles of juice littered the lacquered Chinese dining table and his sixty-four-inch plasma TV was frozen with the image of a smiling purple dinosaur.

And Nathan couldn't seem to get the grin off his face. These past three days had been the richest ones of his life.

Kelly's child was as spirited as she was. He would have loved Jamie simply because Kelly did, but the boy was already working his way into Nathan's heart. He chuckled as he pried the metal car from his bare foot. The boy was working his way into his sole, too.

At the sound of his telephone, Nathan had to pull up the cushions again. He found the phone stuffed into the corner of the couch. "Beliveau here."

"Hi, chief. What the hell did you tell Tony?"

"Hello, Derek. Is something wrong?"

"I thought you settled your debt with him when you offed Volski."

"Yeah, I did. It's paid in full." Nathan plucked a tiny sock from the arm of the couch and sat. "And for the record, the feds are calling Volski's death an accident. That's good enough for me."

"Sure, but I figured your deal was over. Now Tony wants me to tie up your loose end."

"What loose end?"

"The Canyon Brotherhood."

Nathan curled his fingers over the sock in his hand. Templar had dismissed the possibility that the secretive Brotherhood might be a threat to Jamie, but Nathan hadn't wanted to take any chances. Apparently, Tony had shared his concerns. "Don't tell me you're worried you can't handle it, Derek. You told me you were the best."

"Better believe it, chief. But you're going to owe me big-time when I'm done."

"Whatever it takes," Nathan said.

He finished cleaning up and walked to the bedroom Kelly had chosen for Jamie. As he'd done every night since they'd moved in, he paused in the doorway and listened to her sing. She'd chosen an old Simon and Garfunkel song for a lullaby tonight. Her voice was soft, hardly above a whisper, yet the strength of her emotions filled the room like a symphony.

Sometimes the love he felt for her still scared him,

but not as much as the prospect of what his life might have been if he hadn't found her. "Kelly?"

She tucked the blanket around Jamie, kissed his cheek and tiptoed to the doorway. Smiling, she slipped her hand into Nathan's. "Yes, my love?"

He thought about the jeweler's box in his pocket. He'd chosen the ring this afternoon and had planned a romantic dinner that had somehow turned into cookies and juice. He tugged her into the hall. "Say that again."

"What? Yes?"

"Good answer," he murmured.

"What was the question?"

"I'll tell you later," he said, brushing her lips with his. "Much later."

* * * * *

There's more PAYBACK!
Don't miss the exciting conclusion of
Ingrid Weaver's thrilling miniseries.
ROMANCING THE RENEGADE
October 2005
Only from Intimate Moments!

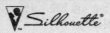

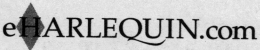

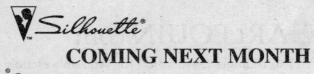

COMING NEXT MONTH